S0-ABO-635

A SHAFT OF SUNLIGHT

Giōna had not slept well because she had sensed when the Duke had said goodnight that something had annoyed him. "What has . . . upset him? What could . . . I have . . . done?" she asked herself. Then she went over it in her mind.

The Duke had kissed his grandmother's cheek and walked towards the front door. He had not yet spoken to Giōna. He was at the door when she said wistfully: "Goodnight . . . Your Grace."

He did not look at her, nor turn his head. He merely replied: "Goodnight!" as if he were speaking from the icy reaches of the North Pole. He drove away, and Giōna, watching until the carriage was out of sight, felt as if it carried her heart with it.

It was not until several hours later in the darkness of her bedroom that she admitted to herself that she loved the Duke. "I love him! I love him!" she whispered into her pillow. She tossed and turned until the first golden fingers of dawn crept up the sky. It was only then that she fell asleep, with the word "love" still on her lips.

Bantam Books by Barbara Cartland
Ask your bookseller for the books you have missed

**A NEW SERVICE FOR
BARBARA CARTLAND READERS**

Now you can have the latest Barbara Cartland romances delivered to your home automatically each month. For further information on this new reader service, contact the Direct Response Department, Bantam Books, 666 Fifth Avenue, New York, N. Y. 10103. Phone (212) 765-6500

A
Shaft
of
Sunlight

Barbara Cartland

BANTAM BOOKS
TORONTO · NEW YORK · LONDON · SYDNEY

A SHAFT OF SUNLIGHT
A Bantam Book / December 1981

All rights reserved
Copyright © 1981 by Barbara Cartland.
This book may not be reproduced in whole or in part, by
mimeograph or any other means, without permission.
For information address: Bantam Books, Inc.

ISBN 0-553-20234-0

Published simultaneously in the United States and Canada

Bantam Books are published by Bantam Books, Inc. Its trade-
mark, consisting of the words "Bantam Books" and the por-
trayal of a rooster, is Registered in U.S. Patent and Trademark
Office and in other countries. Marca Registrada. Bantam
Books, Inc., 666 Fifth Avenue, New York, New York 10103.

PRINTED IN THE UNITED STATES OF AMERICA

0 9 8 7 6 5 4 3 2 1

Author's Note

If was after the development of the Sugar Plantations that the slave-trade between the West Coast of Africa and the Americas reached enormous proportions, becoming the most lucrative trade of the time.

The English became the most important importers of slaves, although the Dutch, the French, and other nations also took part in the trade.

Ships set out first from a home port such as Liverpool, carrying liquor, cotton goods, fire-arms, and trinkets, which were exchanged for slaves right along what was called the Slave Coast—the Gulf of Guinea.

Then came what was known as "the middle voyage" towards one of the Colonies or countries on the American continent. The slaves, closely packed in the hull and often chained to prevent them from rebelling or jumping into the sea, suffered agonies.

Food was inadequate, water was scarce, and mortality often reached the appalling proportion of twenty percent. If it was necessary to reduce the load in a heavy sea, the sick were thrown overboard.

On arrival, slaves were kept in stockades to await a purchaser. The ship was then loaded with another cargo, such as sugar produced on the American plantations, and sailed for home. If all went well, the profit was enormous.

Despite strong protests against this traffic by the

Quakers and William Wilberforce, it was not until 1806 that Parliament prohibited British Merchants from providing slaves and the importation of them into British possessions.

The traffic continued, however, until 1811 when slave-trading became a criminal offence.

Chapter One

1819

The Butler at Alverstode House in Grosvenor Square was surprised to see the Viscount Frome alighting from his Phaeton.

His surprise was not connected with His Lordship's appearance, because he was used to such resplendence, knowing the Viscount's ambition was to be the most acclaimed "Tulip of Fashion" in the *Beau Monde*.

However, what was astonishing was that the twenty-one-year-old Ward of the Duke of Alverstode had appeared so early in the morning.

Barrow was well aware that like the rest of the Dandies the Viscount rose late and spent at least two hours preparing himself to face a critical world.

Yet now when the hands of the clock had not reached nine the Viscount was walking up the steps towards him.

"Good-morning, M'Lord!" Barrow said. "You've come to see His Grace?"

"I am not too late?" the Viscount asked anxiously.

"No, indeed, M'Lord. His Grace returned from riding but ten minutes ago, and Your Lordship'll find him in the Breakfast-Room."

1

The Viscount did not wait to hear any more, but walked across the impressive marble Hall towards the Breakfast-Room which overlooked the garden at the back of the house.

As he expected, the Duke of Alverstode was seated at a table in the window, with *The Times* propped up in front of him on a silver stand while he ate a hearty breakfast with which he drank coffee.

As the Viscount walked into the room, the Duke looked up with the same expression of surprise as had appeared on his Butler's face.

"Good-morning, Cousin Valerian," the Viscount said.

"Good Heavens, Lucien! What brings you here at this early hour? Can you have been engaged in a duel that you have risen so early?"

"No, certainly not!" the Viscount replied sharply, before he realised that his Guardian was merely teasing him.

He crossed the room to sit down on the other side of the table. Then there was a silence which told the Duke without it being put into words that his Ward was nervous.

"If it was not a duel," he remarked after eating another mouthful of the lamb-chop which was in front of him, "then what can be perturbing you?"

Again there was silence before, almost as if the words burst from his lips, the Viscount replied:

"I am in love!"

"Again?" the Duke exclaimed, pausing in his eating.

"This is different!" the Viscount replied. "I know I have thought myself to be in love before, but this is very, very different."

"In what way?" the Duke enquired.

The tone of his voice made the Viscount look at him apprehensively.

There was no doubt that his Guardian was an extremely handsome man, but he was also an awesome one, and there was nobody in the whole of the *Beau*

Monde who did not treat the Duke of Alverstode with respect.

Even the women who pursued him, and there were a great many of them, admitted when they were confidential with one another that they found him a little frightening.

Even The Regent was known to conform to the Duke's opinion and seldom contradicted anything he said.

"I want to marry Claribell," the Viscount said after a pause, "but you made me promise I would not propose marriage to anybody until I had your permission."

"A very wise precaution on my part," the Duke said drily. "I cannot believe you would be very happy if I had allowed you to marry that Don's daughter who took your fancy when you were at Oxford, or that Opera-Dancer who you assured me at the time was the love of your life."

"I was very young then," the Viscount replied hastily.

"You are not so very old now."

"I am old enough to know my own mind!" the Viscount retorted. "I know I shall be exceedingly happy with Claribel, and at least you cannot say she is 'common,' which is how you referred to the other ladies who have engaged my attention."

The Duke raised his eye-brows.

"'Ladies'?" he queried, and it was an insult.

"Have it your own way," the Viscount said petulantly. "They were not 'up to scratch,' as you pointed out to me in no uncertain terms, but you can hardly cut off my money as you threatened to do then because I want to marry Claribel, because for one thing she has a fortune of her own."

"That is always useful," the Duke conceded, "but tell me more about this new enchantress who has captured your somewhat vacillating heart."

The Viscount needed no encouragement. He bent

forward eagerly in his chair, his elbows on the table, to
say:

"She is beautiful—so beautiful that she makes me
think she has stepped down from Olympus—and yet
she loves me! Can you believe it? She loves me for
myself!"

The Duke's expression was rather more cynical than
usual and he looked across the table thinking that a
great number of women had already thought themselves in love with his Ward, and he was certain there
would be a great many more.

The Viscount's father was a distant cousin who had
been killed at Waterloo, and it had been a distinct and
not particularly pleasant shock for the Duke to find
that he had become the Guardian of his son.

He was aware that the late Viscount Frome's Will
had been made some years earlier while his own father
was still alive.

It had simply stated that if anything happened to him
while he was on active service with Wellington's Army,
his son and any other children he might have were to
become Wards of the Duke of Alverstode.

The Duke had often thought it was a careless omis-
sion on the part of the Solicitors who had drawn up his
cousin's Will not to have named his father as the third
Duke.

This would have meant that he himself could have
passed on what was undoubtedly a tiresome duty to
some other member of the family.

At the same time, because he was legally Lucien's
Guardian, he was determined to see that the boy did
not make what was in his opinion a disastrous marriage.

There was no doubt that everybody who had engaged
or captured the Viscount's attention up to date had
been from a social point of view completely unacceptable.

There had been not only the two ladies already
mentioned but also, the Duke remembered, a socially

ambitious widow several years older than Lucien who had fancied herself a Viscountess.

Besides these there had been a lady of very doubtful virtue who had tried to make a great deal of trouble about her "broken heart," which fortunately had been most successfully mended when she received a large number of golden sovereigns.

"Your eulogy of this mysterious creature of mythology is very touching," the Duke said mockingly, "but so far you have omitted to tell me her name."

"She is Claribel Stamford," the Viscount said in a rapt voice.

He saw the frown of concentration on the Duke's face as he tried to remember where he had heard the name.

"Stamford," he said after a moment. "You do not mean that she is the daughter of Sir Jarvis Stamford, the race-horse owner?"

"That is right," the Viscount said. "I thought you would remember him. He owns some excellent horse-flesh, and if you recall he pipped one of your horses to the post last year in the Cambridgeshire."

"Victorious was off-colour that day!" the Duke said defensively, then laughed as he added:

"I remember now that Stamford was certainly remarkably elated at beating me."

"Even so, there is no need for you to be prejudiced against his daughter."

"I have not said I am prejudiced," the Duke protested.

"Then you will allow me to marry her?" the Viscount asked eagerly.

The Duke was silent.

He was thinking that at twenty-one his Ward was still very young and in some ways as ingenuous and, in his opinion, as "hare-brained" as any School-boy.

He had also been very wild and in some people's opinion had sewed a prodigious and unprecedented number of "wild oats."

Not that the Duke thought any the worse of him because of that, for it was what he expected any young man would do when there was no war on which to expend his high spirits, regardless of who was injured in the process.

The Duke was quite certain in his own mind that Claribel, or whatever Lucien's latest infatuation was called, was not likely to prove a more suitable wife than any other of the women who had taken his fancy.

While he was pondering the matter for some time in silence, the Viscount had been watching the Duke's face anxiously, and now he said impetuously:

"If you are going to refuse me permission to pay my addresses to Claribel, Cousin Valerian, I swear I will persuade her to run away with me and damn the consequences!"

The Duke stiffened and said sharply:

"If she is the type of girl you should marry, and certainly the sort of girl to whom I would give my approval, she would refuse to do anything so outrageous!"

He paused before he added:

"No decent girl, and certainly none with any idea of correct behaviour, would contemplate for a moment posting to Gretna Green or being married in some 'hole and corner' manner, which, as you are well aware, is only a type of blackmail on those who hold your best interests at heart."

The Viscount threw himself back in his chair in a sulky manner.

"Now that I am twenty-one I thought I was allowed to be a man, not a puppet tied to your apron-strings!"

The Duke's rather hard mouth twitched.

"A rather mixed metaphor, my dear Lucien," he said, "but I get your meaning."

"You certainly treat me as if I were in petticoats," the Viscount complained.

"Strange though it may seem," the Duke replied, "if I do, I am thinking of your interests and yours only. But I will certainly admit that Miss Stamford sounds a better proposition than anything you have suggested previously."

There was a new light in the Viscount's eyes.

"Then you will consider my request?"

"Most certainly!" the Duke replied.

Once again the Viscount was bending forward eagerly.

"You had best meet Claribel, and then you will understand why I wish to make her my wife."

"That is just what I was about to suggest," the Duke said, "and I always think it is best to see people at their own home and against their natural background."

"You mean . . . ?" the Viscount asked hesitatingly.

"I suggest you ask Sir Jarvis if he is prepared to invite you and me to stay with him for a day or so."

"In the country?"

"Definitely in the country!" the Duke said firmly.

The Viscount looked at his Guardian uncertainly.

"I cannot quite understand, Cousin Valerian, why you think that is important."

"Must I make explanations?" the Duke asked. "I should have thought my reasons were obvious."

"Sir Jarvis has a house in London and Claribel enjoys attending Balls that are taking place there at the moment."

"I am sure she does," the Duke replied, "and as you dance very prettily she doubtless finds you an admirable partner."

He did not make it sound a compliment, and the Viscount, who fancied himself on the dance-floor, flushed a little resentfully. Then he said,

"If I suggest a visit to the country and Sir Jarvis does not wish to leave London, what shall I do?"

"I think," the Duke said loftily, "you will find Sir Jarvis will be only too agreeable to the suggestion of inviting me to be his guest. If, on the other hand, he prefers to wait indefinitely before issuing such an invitation, then, you, my dear Lucien, must wait too."

There was something in the way the Duke spoke which told the Viscount there would be no point in arguing further.

At the same time, he was worried in case Claribel, who loved London, would not wish to return to the country.

His thoughts were very obvious to the Duke, who however, had returned to his perusal of the *Times* turning the newspaper over on its silver rack and drinking his coffee as he read it, apparently no longer interested in his Ward.

The Viscount did not speak for a few minutes. Then he said hesitatingly:

"I suppose, Cousin Valerian, I should thank you for not having given me a complete set-down. I am sure when you meet Claribel you will understand what I feel about her."

"I am sure I shall," the Duke replied.

He finished his coffee, put down the cup, and pushing back his chair rose to his feet.

"And now," he said, "I have a great deal of work to do. What really worries me is what you will find to occupy yourself with until your friends, who I believe seldom wake before noon, are capable of receiving you."

"You are laughing at me," the Viscount replied in an annoyed tone.

"Not really," the Duke replied. "I do not think it is a laughing matter that you take so little exercise except on the dance-floor, and the only fresh air you breathe is between your lodgings in Half Moon Street and your Club!"

"That is not true!" the Viscount answered hotly. "Yesterday I went to a Mill at Wimbledon and last week—or was it the week before—I attended the races at Epsom."

"What I was really suggesting," the Duke said patiently, "was that you should ride every morning or, if you prefer, later in the day. I have always told you that my horses are at your disposal."

"I really do not seem to have the time," the Viscount replied.

"Or if you do not want to ride," the Duke went on as if he had not spoken, "a few strenuous rounds at 'Gentleman Jackson's Boxing Academy' will develop the muscles of your arms and doubtless improve your general stamina."

"I loathed boxing at Eton! I have no desire for anybody to knock me about!" the Viscount exclaimed passionately.

Then looking at the Duke he added:

"It is all very well for you, Cousin Valerian, because you are a natural athlete. Everybody says that, and you are better at boxing and fencing—and riding, for that matter—than most other people."

"I am only better because I have taken the trouble to learn the art of the first two sports you have mentioned," the Duke explained, "and I ride because I love horses, besides the fact that the exercise keeps me fit."

"I prefer driving," the Viscount remarked petulantly.

"A lazy sport, but of course you can always have an audience to admire your expertise with the reins."

"Now you are trying to make a fool of me!" the Viscount complained bitterly.

The Duke sighed.

Then he said in a very different tone:

"Not really. As a matter of fact, Lucien, I am thinking of you and trying to help you to the best of my ability to be the sort of man your father would have wanted you to be. Perhaps I am making a mess of it, but then I have not had much practice at being the Guardian of anybody!"

The way he spoke without appearing cynical or mocking swept the sulky, resentful look from the Viscount's eyes.

"I am—not ungrateful, Cousin Valerian, for the way you have treated me since Papa died. You have been very generous about everything I have wanted to do except where it has concerned marriage."

"Then let us hope," the Duke answered, "that this time I shall be able to give my whole-hearted approval to the lady of your choice."

"You will—I know you will!" the Viscount said eagerly. "Wait until you see Claribel! You will be bowled over by her!"

He gave the Duke a somewhat bashful smile as he added:

"What I am afraid of is that when she meets you she may prefer you to me! She has already told me she has admired you from a distance."

"I am gratified!" the Duke said drily. "At the same time, Lucien, the one thing that need not trouble you in the slightest is that I shall take Claribel or any other very young women from you. For one thing I find them a dead bore, and secondly I have no intention of marrying, not for many years, at any rate."

"You have to produce an heir to the Dukedom sooner or later," the Viscount remarked.

"There is plenty of time for that when I think I am growing senile," the Duke replied. "Then doubtless there will be somebody who will be prepared to provide me with a son and support me in my dotage!"

The Viscount laughed.

"There is no question of that! Your reputation as a heart-breaker, Cousin Valerian, loses nothing in the telling!"

The Duke frowned.

It was the sort of remark that he thought was in extremely bad taste, and he was quite certain that it had been made to Lucien by the women with whom he usually associated.

As if he knew he had presumed on his Guardian's unexpected good humour, the Viscount said hastily:

"If you have work to do, though I cannot conceive what it could be, I will leave you. My Phaeton is outside."

"The new one?" the Duke exclaimed. "I saw the bill for it yesterday. You are certainly determined to cut a dash in more ways than one!"

"Those Coach-builders are all crooks," the Viscount said, "but actually you cannot imagine what a slap-up vehicle it is and how fast it can travel. If you will come and look at it, Cousin Valerian, you will know that what I am saying is the truth."

"I will keep that treat for another day," the Duke replied, "but now Middleton is waiting for me and we have a great deal to do before I have luncheon at Carlton House."

"I am going," the Viscount said. "I will see Sir Jarvis sometime today and try to persuade him to arrange a date for our visit to Stamford Towers."

"I shall be waiting to receive his invitation," the Duke answered. "Until then, good-bye, Lucien!"

He did not listen for his Ward's reply, but walked swiftly from the Breakfast-Room down the corridor towards his Library, where he knew his Secretary and Comptroller would be waiting for him.

For a few seconds the Viscount watched him go, thinking that on the whole the interview had not been as terrifying as he had thought it might be, and also envying almost unconsciously the athletic and co-ordinated manner in which the Duke moved.

It was almost, he thought, like watching a thorough-bred gallop past the Winning-Post, and just for a moment he toyed with the idea of doing what his Guardian suggested and taking more exercise.

Then he was sure that to do so would only prove conclusively what he knew already, that it was impossible for him to excell at sports and he had better spend his time with his tailor and on the dance-floor.

He walked across the Hall to where Barrow was waiting to hand him his tall hat and his riding-gloves.

"Everything all right, Master Lucien?" he asked in the conspiratorial tone of a servant who had known him ever since he was a small boy.

"It might have been worse!"

"I'm glad about that, Master Lucien."

"Thank you, Barrow."

The Viscount smiled at the old retainer and walking down the steps climbed into his Phaeton, which he thought with pride was smarter than anything that could be seen in the Park or anywhere else in London.

It had cost a lot of money, but he could afford it, the only drawback being that all his extravagances still had to be seen and approved by his Guardian before the bills were paid.

The Viscount asked himself as he had a thousand times before why his father had tied up his considerable fortune until he was twenty-five.

Most men, he thought hotly, handled their own money when they came of age! But no, not him! He had to be spoon-fed for another four years! And he found it extremely irksome.

Then he remembered that Claribel would be waiting to hear the result of his visit and he forgot about everything else.

He wished it could be possible to call on her immediately and tell her what the Duke had said, but he knew there could be no possibility of seeing her until nearly luncheon-time and it would be more correct to call later in the afternoon.

"I cannot wait as long as that!" the Viscount told

himself, and thought it was agony to hang about in suspense.

It was not surprising that he was enamoured of one of the most beautiful girls who had ever appeared in a London Season.

It was not only, as the Viscount thought poetically, that her hair was like sunshine, her eyes as blue as a thrush's egg, and her skin like strawberries and cream. It was also that she had none of the gaucheness of the usual débutante.

Perhaps it was her beauty that gave her an assurance and a composure that was lacking in all the other young girls he had met.

'With my money and hers,' the Viscount was thinking as he drove his horses into Park Lane, 'we can live in a really slap-up style. I will be able to give Claribel anything she desires, besides having horses to ride that will be the envy of every man in St. James's!'

* * *

Seated at his desk in the Library, which was piled with papers, while Mr. Middleton explained some complicated problem which had arisen on one of the Alverstode Estates, the Duke found his mind wandering to Lucien.

He felt, as he had so often before, worried about the boy.

He was convinced that the Visount's friends were an exceptionally brainless collection of young men, but he recognised that perhaps he was being over-critical because he was so much older than they were.

"I cannot believe I was as bird-witted when I was twenty-one," he told himself.

But he had been in the Army then, and now not every young man with intelligence, drive, and courage had the same chance to excell as he had enjoyed.

As Mr. Middleton finished his long discourse on the

necessity for completing a new timber-yard and a road leading to it, the Duke said:

"I am worried about Mr. Lucien. What have you heard about him lately?"

Mr. Middleton had been with the Duke for so long that Lucien was usually still referred to as he had been before he came into the title.

Mr. Middleton paused before he replied:

"I do not think His Lordship has done anything particularly outrageous in the last few months. There have been the usual stories about him and his friends being rowdy in dance-halls."

He paused, saw that the Duke was listening, and went on:

"They were thrown out of one of the more respectable 'Houses of Pleasure' the other evening because they were interfering with 'business,' but apart from a rather dangerous duel between two youngbloods at which His Lordship was a 'second,' there is nothing that need concern Your Grace."

"I suppose you were already aware before I was told about it that Mr. Lucien wishes to get married."

"To Miss Claribel Stamford?"

"Yes. I thought you would be the first to know! But you did not report it to me."

"I did not think it serious enough to worry Your Grace," Mr. Middleton replied. "Miss Stamford has a great many admirers."

"She is a beauty?"

"Undoubtedly, and she has already been acclaimed the Débutante of the Season!"

"An 'Incomparable'!" the Duke remarked sarcastically.

"Not yet," Mr. Middleton answered, "but she may easily receive that accolade when the gentlemen in the Clubs become aware of her."

The Duke looked cynical and Mr. Middleton went on:

"Your Grace must have met Sir Jarvis Stamford on the Race-Course?"

"I believe he is a member of the Jockey Club," the Duke said carelessly, "but I cannot remember actually having made his acquaintance. What do you know about him?"

"Very little, Your Grace, but I can easily find out."

"Do that!" the Duke ordered. "I have a feeling, although I may be wrong, that there was some scandal about him at one time, or was it just a rumour about something that was not particularly sporting? I am guessing! I do not really know."

"Leave it to me, Your Grace. In the meantime, I will also discover why Miss Stamford is favouring His Lordship. When I last heard her name mentioned, it was with someone more important in the running."

The Duke stared reflectively at his Secretary.

"What you are saying, Middleton," he said slowly, "is that Miss Stamford, or perhaps her father, is socially ambitious."

Mr. Middleton smiled.

"Of course, Your Grace. All young ladies are, and as Your Grace well knows, the higher the title the better the catch!"

He saw the Duke's lips tighten and remembered, as the Viscount had, that any mention of his love-affairs annoyed him excessively.

However, he was pursued ardently not only because he was a Duke but because he was an exceedingly attractive man, and his very lofty indifference was a challenge which most women found irresistible.

Surprisingly, in an age of loose talk and even looser morals, the Duke considered it in bad taste to discuss any woman who interested him, even with his closest friends, and this prejudice, which was well known, added to the mystery and the aura which surrounded him almost like a protecting halo.

There was not a woman in the whole of the *Beau Monde* who was not aware that if she could capture the heart of the Duke of Alverstode she would achieve a success greater than that of winning the Derby.

Although the Duke had had many *affaires de coeur,* they were discreet, and even the gossips knew nothing about them until they were over.

Then they could only guess at what had occurred when some well-known beauty retired unexpectedly to the country or went about looking so miserable that it was obvious she had lost something of very great value.

The word "heart-breaker," which the Viscount had injudiciously used, was whispered from *Boudoir* to *Boudoir.*

But because the Duke was so fastidious in his choices, and because the women who loved him were seldom if ever spiteful when he left them, those who were interested in the details of his love-life continued to be frustrated.

Mr. Middleton picked up his papers.

"I will find out everything I can, Your Grace," he said, "and furnish whatever information there is about Sir Jarvis as quickly as possible."

"Thank you, Middleton, I knew I could rely on you."

The Duke rose from the desk at which he had been sitting for nearly two hours and stretched his legs.

"I am going now to Carlton House," he said, "but as I shall doubtless be forced to over-eat and over-drink, which I very much dislike doing in the middle of the day, send a groom to 'Gentleman Jackson's' and tell him I hope to be there about half-after-four and would be obliged if I could have a few rounds with him personally."

Mr. Middleton smiled.

"I am sure he will be willing to oblige Your Grace, despite the fact that I hear you knocked him down last week."

The Duke laughed.

"I think perhaps I was unusually lucky, or Jackson was off his guard, but it was certainly an achievement."

"It was indeed, Your Grace."

As "Gentleman Jackson" had been the greatest boxer ever known, this was undoubtedly true, and there was a reminiscent smile on the Duke's lips as he left the Library.

* * *

It was much later in the day when Sir Jarvis Stamford returned to his large and extremely impressive house in Park Lane.

As he entered the door, where a Butler and six footmen were in attendance, his Secretary, a small, rather harassed man who always spoke in a somewhat hesitant manner, came hurrying towards him.

"Miss Claribel, Sir, asked if you would see her the moment you returned home."

Sir Jarvis gave his Secretary a sharp look as if he suspected there was some special reason behind the message.

Then as he was about to speak he realised that the six footmen, who had all to be of exactly the same height and who wore a very distinguished livery of purple and black, were listening.

"Where is Miss Claribel?" he asked quickly.

"In her own Sitting-Room, Sir."

Sir Jarvis walked up the stairs, his feet sinking into the soft carpet whose pile was deeper and certainly more expensive than the carpets in most other people's homes.

When he reached the top of the staircase Sir Jarvis found himself facing a painting he had recently bought in a Sale-Room and which he had been assured was a Rubens.

He only hoped he had not been crooked on the

purchase, which had been an exceedingly expensive one, and he thought that if he had been, somebody would undoubtedly suffer for it.

He walked down the passage, which was slightly over-filled with expensive furniture, to the very elegant Sitting-Room which adjoined Claribel's bedroom and which had been decorated to be a perfect frame for her beauty.

The white and gold walls, the blue hangings, and the painted ceiling which had been done by an Italian artist would certainly become any woman, and as Claribel sprang from the sofa to run towards her father, he thought she looked like a priceless jewel, with or without the appropriate frame.

"Papa! I am so glad you are back!"

"What has happened?" Sir Jarvis asked almost harshly.

"Lucien has seen the Duke! He has really plucked up the courage at last! But as you know, I have had to bully him into making the effort."

"But you succeeded!"

"Yes, I succeeded!"

Claribel took her father by the hand and led him to the sofa where they sat down side by side.

"Well?" he asked. "What happened?"

Claribel drew in her breath.

"Lucien told the Duke that he wished to marry me."

Sir Jarvis's lips tightened as if he anticipated that his daughter would now say that the request had been refused.

"And what do you think the Duke said?" Claribel asked.

"Tell me."

"He said that he wishes to see me in my home and in the country!"

For a moment Sir Jarvis did not speak. He only stared at his daughter as if he doubted what he had heard. Then he said:

"The Duke wishes to *stay* with us at Stamford Towers?"

Claribel nodded.

"Yes, and I am sure that means, Papa, that he will give his consent. Oh, is it not wonderful? I can be married before the end of the Season, and I shall be able to attend the Opening of Parliament as a Viscountess!"

"And you will be the most beautiful Peeress there, my dearest."

"That was what I thought, Papa, and you must buy me a tiara that is bigger and better than anybody else's."

"Of course, of course!" Sir Jarvis agreed. "But I can hardly credit that the Duke wishes to stay with us."

"Lucien was also surprised, because he told me that the Duke is very fastidious about whom he stays with and accepts the invitations only of his close friends, like the Duke of Bedford and the Duke of Northumberland, and refuses thousands of others."

"We must make sure he does not regret his visit to Stamford Towers!"

"We must make sure that he agrees to my marrying Lucien!"

"Yes, yes, of course, but I think that is what is known as a foregone conclusion."

As he spoke Sir Jarvis thought that Claribel was not so confident.

"Why should he not accept you?" he asked sharply. "You are not only beautiful, my dearest, but you are also rich, and nobody can say that your mother's family are not blue-blooded."

"I wonder if Lucien remembered to tell him about Mama?"

"If he has forgotten I will do it myself," Sir Jarvis said, "and once the Duke is in our home he will have to listen to me."

"Of course, Papa, and send him the invitation right

away. Lucien thought it would be a mistake to allow what he called the 'grass to grow under our feet.'"

"I agree with him," Sir Jarvis said. "The sooner the better. In fact, very definitely the sooner."

He spoke as if he was thinking of something other than his daughter. Then he bent forward and kissed her.

"I am very proud of you, my dearest," he said. "This makes it easy to forget that little set-back we had over the Earl of Dorset."

"I am never going to think of him again!" Claribel cried passionately. "He deceived me, and that I will never forgive!"

"Neither will I," Sir Jarvis agreed. "Make no mistake, I will get even with that young man sooner or later, and he will rue the day he behaved to you as he did."

Claribel jumped to her feet and walked to the mantelpiece to stare at her reflection in the mirror above it.

"How could he?" she asked in a low voice, as if she spoke to herself. "How could he have preferred that pie-faced Alice Wyndham to me?"

"Forget it! Forget it!" her father said behind her. "I know young Lucien is only a Viscount, but he is the Ward of the most influential man not only in the Social World but also on the Turf and in the country. The Alverstode Estate is a model for all other great Landowners, and an invitation to stay at Alverstode House is more prized than being asked to any of the Royal Palaces!"

"Then that is where we shall undoubtedly stay not once but frequently," Claribel said in rapturous tones.

"And I hope you will make sure that your poor Papa is included in some of the parties," Sir Jarvis said.

"But of course, Papa! And I feel that once Lucien and I are married, you and the Duke will become close friends. After all, between you, you own all the best race-horses in England."

"Not all, my dear, but certainly a great number of them," Sir Jarvis said complacently.

"And that is a real bond in common, is it not?"

"Of course, of course," Sir Jarvis agreed, "but the closest bond of all will be when you are married to the Duke's Ward, a young man with whom I understand His Grace has deeply concerned himself every since he was a School-boy."

"That is true," Claribel agreed, "and although Lucien is nervous of the Duke he certainly admires him."

"As do a lot of other people!" Sir Jarvis approved. "I think, my dearest, that your future is exactly as I planned it, and you are a very lucky girl."

Claribel turned round from the contemplation of her reflection in the mirror and walked towards her father.

She lifted her face to his, looking so lovely as she did so that he stared at her as if he had never seen her before.

"I shall enjoy being a Viscountess!" she said simply.

Chapter Two

Looking round what was more a Baronial Hall than a Dining-Room, the Duke thought that Sir Jarvis Stamford certainly lived in style.

He had not expected Stamford Towers to be quite so big or to find that inside it was furnished opulently but with good taste.

However, he thought there were an unnecessary number of footmen in the Hall and he was quite certain that his valet would tell him about the army of servants that existed in the kitchen-quarters.

At the moment he was sizing up the guests who had been invited for dinner tonight as highly respectable, and Sir Jarvis himself as a very genial host.

The Duke was well aware that for him to stay with somebody with whom he had a bare acquaintance was unprecedented, and the effusive manner with which he was greeted and Sir Jarvis's anxiety that he should be provided with every comfort were no more than he had expected.

When he had seen Claribel for the first time he had understood why Lucien was in love, for she was without doubt one of the loveliest young women he had ever seen.

At the same time, for his Ward's sake he was deter-

mined to be highly critical, as he still thought that
Lucien was too young to be married.

If he was, it should be to a very exceptional wife who
would help him to develop the better qualities of his
character and dispense with the undesirable ones.

That, the Duke told himself cynically, would undoubtedly be beyond the powers of any girl as young as
Claribel.

However, he had learnt before coming to Stamford
Towers that since she was in mourning for her mother, Miss Stamford had not been presented at Court
last year but had been obliged to wait until this Season before she could appear and dazzle the Social
World.

It was therefore understandable to the Duke that
Claribel appeared to have none of the shyness and
sense of insecurity that was usual in a very young
débutante but had already a poise which would not
have been amiss in a much older woman.

But that did not prevent her from looking as fresh as
a dew-drop and every young man's ideal of spring.

Her extremely expensive white gown was exactly
what a sweet young maiden should wear, and the blue
ribbons which crossed over her breasts and cascaded
down her back were the colour of her eyes.

As course succeeded course, all brought to the table
on gold dishes, the Duke became aware that Sir Jarvis
employed an exceptionally good Chef and the wines
were superlative.

There was certainly no question, he told himself, of
his Ward being married for his money.

But he was still remembering that Mr. Middleton
had said that all young girls were socially ambitious and
the higher the title the better the catch.

Mr. Middleton had also hinted that there had been a
man of greater social importance in Miss Stamford's
orbit, and a few discreet enquiries at White's Club had

enabled the Duke to learn that this was the Earl of
Dorset.

He had met him several times and thought him a
well-mannered, rather serious young man who was a
credit to the Household Cavalry.

But the Duke had learnt that he had sheered off and
married a girl who preferred the country to London and
whose father's Estate marched with his own.

'That was sensible,' he thought.

At the same time, he wondered if there had been
some undisclosed reason for the Earl continuing his
pursuit of the exquisitely lovely Claribel.

As dinner progressed, the Duke saw Lucien staring
at his young hostess with what he termed "sheep's
eyes," and he thought that perhaps he was being too
critical in looking for flaws in such perfection instead of
giving without more ado his whole-hearted consent to
the alliance.

In the years during which he had shown himself to
be an outstandingly brilliant soldier and in the subsequent years of peace, he had learnt to sum up people
quickly and to trust his instinct.

Strangely enough, for no apparent reason he could
possibly ascertain, his instinct at the moment was giving
him warning signals that everything was not quite right.

He had no idea what it was.

He only knew perceptively, as he had known in Spain
and in France when he and his men were in danger
before there was any eveidence of it, that he had to be
on his guard.

"I am being ridiculous," he told himself, and concen-
trated on the conversation of the lady on his right,
whom he found attractive and quite surprisingly intelligent.

When the ladies had retired to the Drawing-Room,
the gentlemen lingered for only a short time over their
port.

The conversation was all on horses, because besides

the Duke and Sir Jarvis there were several other distinguished race-horse owners present.

They talked of their triumphs and ambitions, which the Duke found distinctly interesting.

He was actually reluctant to leave the Dining-Room, were it not that he was aware that Lucien was fidgeting to go and Sir Jarvis was only too willing to make it easy for him to be with Claribel.

In the huge Drawing-Room, which was hung with a number of paintings the Duke would have been delighted to add to his own collection, there were card-tables for those who wished to gamble, comfortable sofas for those who preferred to converse, and one of the guests was playing the piano in an almost professional manner.

The Duke saw Lucien gravitating towards Claribel like a homing pigeon, and, not wishing to embarrass them, he walked out onto the terrace.

The sun was beginning to sink in a blaze of glory and the colour of the sky behind the huge oak trees in the Park was very beautiful.

Behind him the Duke heard Sir Jarvis settling the other guests down at the card-tables and decided he had no wish to gamble.

Instead, he walked over the velvet-smooth lawns, finding that the garden, like the house, was almost too perfect to be real, and he wondered vaguely how many gardeners were employed.

"It must cost Sir Jarvis a pretty penny," the Duke ruminated, and made a mental note to find out where so much money came from.

The invitation to stay at Stamford Towers had arrived so promptly that Mr. Middleton had not had time to bring him the information he required.

He decided that there were a great many questions to be answered before he finally made up his mind to allow Lucien to propose to the delectable Claribel.

He walked on, moving between two yew-hedges that

were clipped until there was not a twig or a leaf
out-of-place, and then he saw ahead of him some steps
that led up by the side of a cascade.

Round the pool there was a blaze of flowers, and
because it was so skilfully planned the Duke walked
curiously up the steps to find at the top a small path
leading through shrubs that were in bloom and whose
fragrance filled the air.

It was so beautiful that he could hardly believe Sir
Jarvis had planned it without a professional designer,
and yet it certainly was a tribute to the character of the
man that he appreciated anything so exceptional.

The Duke walked on and now the shrubs gave way
to pine trees and the path became a mere mossy track
between their trunks.

Through them he could still see the red and gold of
the setting sun and thought that having come so far he
might as well finish his walk by seeing what lay at the
end of the wood.

He had the idea, because Stamford Towers was on
raised ground and this was higher still, that there would
be a fine view, and as the trees thinned until they were
silhouetted against the sky he saw that he had been
right.

At the end of the wood the land dropped down
several hundred feet and there was a view over the
valley which was exceptional.

The Duke stood looking at it, then suddenly he was
aware that he was not alone.

Just a little to the right of him, seated on the trunk
of a fallen tree there was a slight figure.

The Duke was still sheltered by the trees through
which he had been walking, and he realised that the
girl, for that was what she appeared, was not aware of
him.

He thought at first glance that she was probably some
labourer's daughter or perhaps a servant from the house.

She was wearing a grey cotton gown which looked

somewhat like a uniform and she was bending forward as she looked at the view.

He thought that it was rather annoying that he was not alone as he had wished to be and that the best thing he could do would be to turn and go back the way he had come.

Then as if she was conscious of his scrutiny the girl turned her face towards him.

He had the quick impression of huge dark eyes in a small, pale face and was aware that he had been wrong, for she was certainly not a servant but somebody refined and in an unusual way very lovely.

Then as he stared at her she exclaimed:

"How magnificent you are! And just as I thought you would be even though I could only see the top of your head!"

The Duke was astonished.

But before he could find words in which to reply, the girl said:

"I am ... sorry. I ... apologise. I should not have ... said that ... but I was so surprised to see ... you."

The Duke walked the few steps that took him to the fallen tree-trunk and as he did so the girl rose and made him a slight but very graceful curtsey.

"You obviously know who I am," the Duke said, "so it is only fair that you should introduce yourself."

"That is unnecessary."

The Duke raised his eye-brows, then deliberately sat down on the fallen tree-trunk.

"If I have interrupted your communion with nature you must forgive me," he said, "but it is certainly a very beautiful place in which to see the sunset."

She turned her head to look across the valley.

"It is so lovely," she said, "and when I am here I can believe I am seeing the sun set in India."

"India?" the Duke questioned. "You have been there?"

She nodded.

"Tell me about it."

It was half an order and half a plea in a voice that many women had found irresistible.

He realised that she hesitated before she replied:

"I think . . . I should . . . go away."

"Why?" the Duke enquired.

"Because . . . " she began, then she stopped and said, "There is no . . . need for me to . . . explain."

"There is every need," the Duke contradicted. "You could not do anything so infuriating as to go away without explaining why you have only seen the top of my head."

She gave a little gurgle of laughter before she replied:

"That is all one ever sees when one looks down from a top window."

The Duke smiled.

"So you were peeping at me when I arrived!"

"Yes, and through the bannisters on the second floor when you proceeded into dinner."

The Duke was wearing his decorations on his evening-coat because one of the guests at dinner was an obscure foreign Prince, and as she looked at one of them she exclaimed:

"I am sure that is a medal for gallantry."

"How do you know?"

"My father was at one time in the Brigade of Guards."

"Tell me your father's name."

Once again she looked away towards the sunset and did not reply.

"If you will not tell me your father's name," the Duke persisted after a moment, "tell me yours. I find it irritating to converse with somebody who is entirely anonymous."

"If you are so . . . interested, you had better . . . know that I am the . . . skeleton in the cupboard!"

"The skeleton?"

"Exactly! So please, Your Grace, will you promise me on your . . . honour that you will not mention to . . . anybody that you have . . . seen me?"

"It would be very difficult to explain that I had met somebody who had no name and the only thing I knew about her was that she had visited India."

"But you must not . . . say that! They would know . . . at once who I was . . . and it only . . . slipped out because I was so . . . surprised to see . . . you."

"I will give you my promise that I will tell no-one we have met," the Duke said, "if in return you will relieve my curiosity by telling me who you are and why you are here."

She looked at him with her large eyes which the Duke thought were very expressive, and he was aware that she was deciding whether or not she could trust him to keep his word.

Then as if something about him reassured her, she said simply:

"My name is . . . Giōna."

"Greek!"

"That is clever of you!"

"Not really. I used to be fairly proficient at Greek when I was at Oxford, and I visited the country two years ago."

"Did it thrill you? Did you feel as if the gods were still there and the light had not changed since Homer wrote of it?"

"Of course!"

"I had an idea you would . . . feel all those . . . things," she said almost beneath her breath.

"And now tell me why you are here and what connection you have with Stamford Towers," the Duke said.

The expression that had been in her eyes when she spoke of Greece changed dramatically.

"That is a . . . question you must not . . . ask," she said quickly. "I have told you that I am the . . . skeleton in the . . . cupboard."

"In Sir Jarvis's cupboard?"

"Please . . ." she pleaded.

"If you have deliberately set out to intrigue me and

make me so curious that I shall not be able to sleep," the Duke said, "then you have, Giōna, succeeded."

"You promised to . . . forget that you had ever . . . met me!"

"I promised nothing of the sort! I merely said that I would not speak of you to anybody else, and I never break my word of honour."

She smiled.

"That I can believe."

"Then be a little more explicit, in fact a little more kind than you are being at the moment."

"You are making everything very . . . difficult for . . . me," she said. "At the same time . . . although I believe I am dreaming . . . it is very . . . exciting to sit here . . . talking to you. When I heard you were coming to . . . stay, I could hardly . . . believe it."

"You have heard of me before?"

"Yes. Papa was interested in your . . . successes on the . . . Race-Course and many years ago he met your father at a Regimental dinner."

"So your father talked about me?"

Giōna nodded.

"Because we lived abroad, he was interested in everyone he had known before he . . . left England."

"Why did you live abroad?"

She did not answer and the Duke said:

"Tell me more about your father."

"What is the point of remembering him now when he is . . . dead?"

There was a tremor in Giōna's voice which was almost a sob.

She turned her face away so that the Duke should not see the sudden mistiness in her eyes.

"Was your father killed in the war?" the Duke asked gently.

She shook her head.

"No . . . he died . . . and so did . . . Mama, of typhoid in . . . Naples . . . two years . . . ago."

"I am sorry."

"If only I had . . . died with . . . them!"

It was a cry that seemed to burst from her lips.

"You must not speak like that," the Duke said. "You are very beautiful, and life can be an exciting thing, even though for everybody there are ups and downs."

"For me it is very . . . very . . . down. I am in the . . . depths of . . . despair and there is no . . . escape!"

"Why?"

There was silence and after a moment the Duke asked:

"Did your father leave you penniless so that you are forced to work for your living?"

He thought that must be the explanation of why he had mistaken her for a servant and why her grey cotton gown seemed very much the sort of dress a maid would wear.

Then as if she had been insulted Giōna answered angrily:

"Papa provided for me! He would never . . . never have left me . . . penniless! In fact he left me very . . . wealthy!"

The Duke raised his eye-brows.

He could not help looking again at the gown she was wearing, and he could see that peeping beneath the hem her black slippers were worn at the toes.

"Do stop asking questions," she said suddenly. "You will . . . leave me . . . unhappy and make me . . . remember the . . . past . . . which I am . . . trying . . . to forget."

There was something very pathetic in the way she spoke, but before the Duke could reply she added quickly:

"I cannot think why we . . . started this . . . conversation . . . and although it has been more . . . wonderful than I can possibly tell you to . . . talk to you . . . please . . . go away."

"I have no wish to do that," the Duke said firmly.

"But . . . you must . . . you must!" Giōna said. "Besides . . . they might . . . miss you."

"If they do, I shall have a very reasonable explanation for my absence."

"Then I must . . . go," she said, "and please . . . if you want to . . . stay, please do not . . . look at me as I . . . go."

The words came hesitatingly and the Duke stared at her in surprise.

"You must first give me an explanation for your asking that," he said.

He thought Giōna was about to refuse, and he added:

"Otherwise you will make me once again curious, and I shall certainly watch you vanishing between the trees."

"Do you . . . always get your . . . own way?" she asked.

"Invariably!" the Duke replied.

"Then it is very . . . bad for you . . . but I suppose it is to be expected . . . since you are so important and so clever."

"Are you flattering me?" he enquired.

She shook her head.

"The opinion of somebody as insignificant as myself would doubtless be dismissed by a wave of your hand."

The Duke laughed.

"Now you are deliberately trying to provoke me. So let us get back to the question you have not answered— why I should not watch you leave, if that is what you insist on doing."

There was a hint of mischief in Giōna's eyes as if she found it amusing to whet his curiosity even further.

"If you want the truth . . . it is because I have . . . undone the back of my . . . gown and it would be distinctly . . . immodest to move away until I can do it . . . up again."

"Why have you done that?" the Duke asked.

"Are you still . . . interested in hearing the . . . truth?"

"You know I am. Just as you are aware that you are making me more and more inquisitive."

"About a skeleton in a cupboard? Your Grace should

have more important things to occupy your mind."

"It would not be so intriguing if it was not so unexpected."

Giōna gave a little chuckle.

"Perhaps that is true. It is the same way that Papa would have thought. Perhaps that was why it was such fun to be with him."

"Then tell me why you have undone your gown."

"I wonder if I do so whether you will be shocked, surprised, or disgusted."

"I will tell you my reaction when I hear your explanation."

"Very well," Giōna said with a sigh. "Some of the weals on my back are bleeding, and when they . . . stick to my . . . gown it is very . . . painful to pull it off. I also find the evening air . . . cooling."

The Duke stared at her incredulously.

"What are you saying?" he asked.

"I am telling you that I have recently been beaten!" Giōna replied defiantly. "It is something that happens frequently since I came here. Now do you understand why I wish I could have . . . died with . . . Papa and Mama in Naples?"

It was impossible to hide the tears in her eyes, and as they overflowed she wiped them away almost angrily with the back of her hand.

"It is . . . your fault for making me . . . talk like this," she said accusingly. "But it is . . . two years since I have . . . spoken to a man like you."

She drew in her breath before she went on:

"Because you have brought back the happiness I have . . . lost . . . I do not know whether to . . . thank Your Grace . . . the fates . . . or the gods who brought you here this evening."

"Who has beaten you?"

The question came sharply in the authoritative voice which, when the Duke used it, invariably commanded obedience.

There was a little pause before Giōna said in a low voice:

"The same person who . . . brought me here . . . from Naples . . . who defamed my darling mother . . . and who hates me!"

Without her saying any more the Duke knew the answer.

"I presume," he said, "You mean Sir Jarvis?"

Giōna did not speak, but he thought there was a slight affirmative movement of her head.

"Why? What is his connection with you?"

"You gave me your . . . word that . . . nothing we have said will go any further . . . but if you do speak of it . . . he will . . . kill me! He will do it anyway . . . with his floggings . . . but it would be a rather quicker death . . . than the way he is . . . doing it now."

The Duke put out his hand and took Giōna's in his.

"Look at me, Giōna."

Again it was a command, and slowly she turned her face towards him.

There were tears on her cheeks and her eyes were misty, but she still looked lovely in a manner that the Duke was sure was not English but Greek.

"Trust me," he said quietly. "You have told me so much. Trust me with the whole story, and I swear that somehow I will help you."

He felt her fingers tighten on his as if she suddenly felt he was a lifeline to which she could cling.

Then she said helplessly:

"Even if I . . . tell you . . . there is . . . nothing you . . . can do."

"How can you be sure?"

"He will . . . never let me go . . . I am not being hysterical or exaggerating when I say he . . . wants me to . . . die! Then . . . since Papa is . . . dead . . . his secret will be safe forever!"

She spoke in a way that told the Duke irrefutably that she was speaking the truth.

He was a very good judge of character, and he knew
when a man or a woman was being sincere or was
acting or exaggerating in any way.

He was utterly convinced that Giōna was neither
acting nor exaggerating, and again he said as his fingers
tightened on hers:

"Start from the beginning and tell me the whole
story."

"I cannot really start at the ... beginning," Giōna
replied, "because I do not ... know it ... myself."

"Who was your father?"

"Uncle Jarvis's brother."

"So your name is Stamford."

"Yes, but I am not allowed to use it."

"Why not?"

"I am not quite ... certain. Papa used many names as
we ... travelled about, but I know it was something to
do with Uncle Jarvis which made Papa move from
country to country and change his name."

"And your mother went with him?"

"Of course Mama went with him. She loved him.
They loved each other. She would have walked bare-
foot to the top of the Himalayas if he had wanted her
to."

"But he had no money."

"Papa had plenty of money, in fact he was very rich,
but I think most of what he had to spend came from
Uncle Jarvis. It was always waiting for him in the Bank
of any country we visited, so that we lived very comfortably and were very happy."

"But you did not come back to England?"

"I knew we could not. Sometimes Papa would be
restless and look sort of 'far away,' and Mama and I
knew that he was missing his friends, his hunting and
shooting, and all the other things he had enjoyed before
he went abroad."

"Then what happened?" the Duke enquired.

"We had come back to Europe and were in Greece,

until Papa thought it would be fun to explore Italy again. But when we arrived in Naples there was an epidemic of typhoid!"

The Duke felt Giōna's fingers tremble again in his before she went on:

"It was... horrifying! Everybody was so... ill, and before we could... move out of the... city, first Papa and then Mama... collapsed."

"But you survived."

"Unfortunately!"

There was a long silence, then the Duke prompted:

"What happened then?"

"I was so... upset when Papa and Mama died that I first stayed in the Villa we had rented. The Bank which handled the money which was waiting for Papa wrote to England to tell Uncle Jarvis what had happened. That was how he knew where I... was."

"And I presume he came out to fetch you."

Giōna shut her eyes.

"I do not... want to... talk about it."

"I can help you only if you tell me everything."

"I have already... told you that you... cannot help... nobody can. But if you want me to go on with this... miserable story, I will... do so."

That is what I want you to do."

"Uncle Jarvis arrived and he... told me..."

She stopped, and the Duke knew she found it almost impossible to say the next few words, and when she did speak it was in a whisper.

"He... told me that... Papa and Mama were not... married... I was... illegitimate, or as he put it... a bastard!"

She suddenly pulled her hand from the Duke's to say furiously:

"It is not true! I know it is not true! Papa ran away with Mama because his father wanted him to marry an aristocrat as Uncle Jarvis had done."

"And he refused?"

"He had become engaged to a nobleman's daughter, but then he met Mama."

"And they fell in love?" the Duke prompted.

"They were deeply and completely in love, and as Papa knew his father would never consent to the marriage, he persuaded Mama to elope with him. But they were married . . . I know they were!"

"There must be some record of it, and it should not be hard to find."

"I have no . . . chance of . . . looking for it."

"I could do that for you."

"You could? Or rather . . . would you?"

"That is another thing I will promise you to do."

"Mama's father was the Vicar of a small Parish in Hampshire. I know he did not marry them because the Patron of his living was a friend of my grandfather's, and Mama thought her father might be made to suffer for it. So she and Papa were married, I am sure, at Dover."

"Why do you think that?"

"Because to escape all the fuss there was about Papa breaking off his engagement they went to France."

"And was there a fuss?"

"I think so. I am sure there was, for while they were in France, Uncle Jarvis went to see them and said that Papa was to stay out of England because of the scandal he had caused . . . and there was some other reason also."

Giōna made a helpless little gesture with her hands.

"But that is what I do not know. Papa never told me, but thinking back to some of the things Mama said, I know it was then that Uncle Jarvis began to send them so much money and they began to change their name as they went from country to country."

"And what happened to all the money?"

"Uncle Jarvis told me I was . . . illegitimate and he was . . . ashamed and . . . disgusted that I should even . . .

exist. He said I was not... entitled to any of Papa's money and that it was his by law."

"I am sure that is untrue. Whether you were born in wedlock or not, if he made a Will in your favour the money is yours."

"How can I... prove that? Uncle Jarvis brought me back to England with him and said that I should live here at Stamford Towers but that nobody must... see me... and if I ever attracted... attention to myself he would... beat me until I was... unconsious."

"Why did he beat you today?"

"It was yesterday... just before you... arrived. I very stupidly went to look at the table in the Dining-Room. I had never seen all the gold plate brought out before, and the garlands on the table were th best orchids from the greenhouses... but Uncle Jarvis... caught me... there."

"So he beat you!"

"I think he is glad of any excuse, and he has instructed the servants to half-starve me, so that if I grow weak enought I will... die and he will be... rid of me!"

The Duke was about to say that he could not believe that any man could be so bestial or so ruthless, when as if overcome by what she was saying, Giōna bent forward to put her hands over her eyes.

As she did so the back of her gown, which was unbuttoned, fell open and the Duke could see that on the whiteness of her skin there was a criss-cross of weals.

Some of them were purple as if they were beginning to heal, but other were clotted with blood and showed that they were of more recent origin.

For a moment he could only stare incredulously as if he could not believe what he saw.

Then he felt an anger rising within him that was like a burning fire.

It was what he had felt when on the battlefields of

Portugal he had seen some of the soldiers stripped and mutilated, and had been ready to murder with his own hands those who had perpetrated such atrocities.

Now he knew that his instinct which had told him there was something wrong with Sir Jarvis was not at fault, and he was also aware that somehow he had to save Giōna.

He could see not only the weals on her back but the sharp curve of her spine protruding in a manner which told him all too clearly that she was under-nourished.

Then he knew that it was of first importance to convince her that her confidence in him had not been in vain and that somehow he would save her from the fiend who was attempting to destroy her.

"Listen to me, Giōna," he said.

Obediently like a child she raised her face and he saw that despite the tears on her cheeks she had herself under control.

Once again he took her hand in both of his.

"I want you to trust me," he said very quietly, "and I promise you again on my honour that somehow I will save you and I will prove, because it will make you happy, that your father and mother were married."

For a moment Giōna's eyes were incredulous, then they seemed to catch the last golden light of the setting sun and to shine as brilliantly as the first evening star that was just appearing overhead.

"I knew when I first saw you," she said, "that somehow, in some . . . mysterious way I did not . . . understand, you had been sent to . . . help me."

The Duke, holding her hand, said:

"I am going back to the house, and I will be thinking of what we can do. You must meet me here again tomorrow evening."

"There is a Ball tomorrow evening."

"All the better! It will make it easier for us to meet without anybody being in the least suspicious."

"They might be suspicious if . . . you disappear for a long time. After all, you are the most . . . important guest."

"I think my Ward is that. You know, of course, why we are here?"

"Claribel intends to marry him."

"If I give my permission."

"I gather from what is being said in the house that it is a foregone conclusion."

"On the contrary, I made it clear that I would only consider the question as to whether my Ward should propose to Miss Stamford. I can tell you now quite categorically that there is not the slightest chance of my answer being anything but 'No'!"

"That is wise. She would not make him happy."

"How do you know? Apart from the fact that she is your uncle's daughter?"

"That is a question I would . . . rather not answer."

"I will not press you," the Duke said, "since for the moment my only concern is for you."

"I . . . I did not mean to . . . involve you in my . . . troubles. I had not the slightest idea that I would ever . . . see you except . . . "

" . . . From the top window," the Duke said with a smile. "But we have met, Giōna, and I think it was fate."

He knew that she was trembling, but as she did not speak he asked:

"What is frightening you?"

"I was just . . . thinking how . . . furious Uncle Jarvis would be if he knew I had even . . . spoken to you . . . let alone had this . . . conversation."

"He will not know," the Duke said. "That is why we must be careful."

He rose as he spoke, and because he was still holding her hand he drew Giōna to her feet.

"I am going back now," he said, "and I imagine you have your own way of returning, so there is no reason

why anybody in the house should know we have been
here together."

"I . . . I . . . hope not," Giōna said. "The servants
do not like walking in the woods when it is getting
dark . . . it seems spooky to them . . . and anyway nobody
will miss me."

"Have you had your dinner?"

She gave a little laugh.

"I may . . . or may not find something in my room. I
am not allowed to go to the kitchen when there is a
house-party for fear the valets and lady's-maids belong-
ing to the guests should see me."

"You are too thin!" the Duke observed abruptly
because it upset him to think of her hungry.

Giōna shrugged her shoulders.

"I have been spoilt by the food I ate with Papa and
Mama, who thought cooking was an art . . . and I find it
difficult to eat the remains of the servants' meals, which
is . . . all I have here . . . but there is . . . no alternative."

"There will be in the future," the Duke said, "and
when you go to bed tonight remember, Giōna, that
the future will be as bright and as lovely as the sun
that will rise again in the morning."

"I . . . I want to believe . . . that," she said.

"If you pray, which I have a feeling you do," he said,
"pray that the night and the darkness will pass quickly."

"How can you be so understanding?" she asked.
"That is the sort of thing Papa would have said to me."

"I think the one thing your father would have wanted,"
the Duke said, "would be for you to believe that I am
here to help you."

"I want to believe that . . . but I am . . . afraid!"

"Of your uncle? Forget him!"

She drew in her breath and he knew that she was
thinking of the beating she had received yesterday and
of her uncle's anger if he had the slightest idea she had
revealed so many secrets to the Duke.

"You promised to trust me," the Duke said quietly.

"I do! I swear I do!" Giōna said. "And thank
you . . . thank you for bringing me . . . hope when there
was only . . . darkness and despair."

"That is over and you will soon forget. In the meantime, we have to be very careful, very cautious."

She nodded.

The Duke released her hand.

Then as if there was no need for any more words, as
the last glow of golden light sank over the horizon, he
turned and walked back the way he had come along the
twisting path through the pine wood which led first to
the shrubs, then to the steps beside the cascade.

Then he moved as swiftly as he could, not straight
towards the house but to another part of the garden, so
that when he approached the terrace leading into the
Drawing-Room he came from a different direction alto-
gether.

Now he walked slowly and casually, as if he was deep
in thought, and as he neared the steps which led down
onto the lawn from the terrace he was acutely aware
that somebody was waiting for him behind the grey
stone balustrade.

"So there you are!" Sir Jarvis exclaimed as the Duke
slowly ascended the steps. "I wondered what had become of you!"

"I have been admiring your garden, Stamford," the
Duke said. "It is absolutely delightful! You must tell
me who planned it."

Sir Jarvis laughed.

"I am gratified that it pleases you. Shall I sound very
conceited if I tell you that I laid it all out myself? It is
one of the achievements of which I feel justifiably
proud!"

There was no doubt that his tone of voice echoed that
sentiment.

At the same time, the Duke was aware that he
lied.

Chapter Three

If Giōna stayed awake, finding it impossible to believe what had happened, so did the Duke.

He had made himself particularly pleasant to Sir Jarvis to eliminate any possible suspicion that might be in his mind, and when finally he reached his own bedroom Hibbert was waiting for him and he undressed in silence.

Only when Hibbert was about to leave the room, holding his evening-clothes over his arm, did the Duke say:

"Tell me what you make of this place, Hibbert. I am interested to hear your views."

His valet looked at him enquiringly, being well aware that he would not have asked the question without there being some good reason for it.

He had been batman to the Duke while he was in the Army and had been exceedingly useful on many occasions by obtaining information when they had captured a town or a village which otherwise would not have been available to the English.

Hibbert, despite his very English name, was a mixture of several nationalities, which meant that he found it easy to speak other languages besides his own, and his proficiency both in French and in Portuguese had been invaluable.

Now he hesitated before he said slowly:

"Sir Jarvis, Your Grace, employs a larger number of people than any house we've visited recently, but as Your Grace has asked me my opinion, it's that they're not happy."

"Why not?"

"I'm not quite certain, Your Grace," Hibbert replied, "but there's a sort of undercurrent about everything that makes me think, although I'm sure it's ridiculous, that they're afraid in some way."

"I do not think it ridiculous," the Duke said, "and I want you to try to find out what makes them afraid and anything else that you think might be of interest to me."

He was well aware that there was a alert look in Hibbert's eyes, like that in the eyes of a terrier who scents a rat.

He had often thought that Hibbert, like himself, found peacetime dull, and when the valet had left him he thought that it was in fact the truth.

The superficiality of the Social World, the way in which party succeeded party all much the same and the women showed little originality or individuality, had contrived to make him both bored and cynical.

Now the knowledge that he had not only to save Giōna but to outwit what he was sure would be a formidable enemy resuscitated a feeling he had not known since the defeat of Napoleon had brought an end to the hostilities with France.

He thought over all she had said and built up a picture in his mind.

But he knew that it was not going to be easy to prove why Sir Jarvis had paid large sums of money to his brother to stay abroad unless Middleton could unearth a scandal to account for it.

Try as he would, he could not recall anything other than a vague idea that somehow he had heard something derogatory about Sir Jarvis.

"It must have been a long time ago," he said to himself.

Then he remembered the horror he had felt when he saw the weals on Gīōna's back, and he knew that if it was the last thing he did he would save her from a cruelty which must cause her indescribable agony.

For one thing, it had been impossible not to see the pain she was suffering etched on her face, and he wished he could give Sir Jarvis some of his own medicine and whip him until he was unconscious.

He had felt such a wave of hatred well up inside him when he met his host on the terrace that only years of self-control, which was due in part to his Army training, made the Duke respond to Sir Jarvis's geniality with flattering appreciation of his garden, his house, and his daughter.

It had been, the Duke thought in retrospect, a fine piece of acting, and he only hoped he could continue the role tomorrow without Sir Jarvis having the slightest suspicion that he was not favourably inclined towards an alliance between Claribel and Lucien.

Then as he thought of his Ward he was suddenly aware that it was not going to be easy to convince him that the girl he loved was as reprehensible and despicable as her father.

If he had read Lucien's character right, direct opposition to his plans to marry Claribel would only make him all the more determined to press his suit, with or without his Guardian's approval.

'It is what I would do myself,' the Duke thought with a wry smile.

He knew that in fact it was an admirable trait for any young man to believe in the woman he loved rather than to listen to defamatory hearsay against her .

The Duke was well aware that this constituted another problem and a very definite obstacle which must be overcome if Sir Jarvis was to get his just deserts.

In the same way as he planned every move of his

troops before going into battle, the Duke began to think out his moves one by one, and it was a long time before he got to sleep.

* * *

The Duke had arranged to ride early the next morning before breakfast in the same way that he rode when he was at home in the country or in London.

Hibbert called him at seven and helped him dress in customary silence before the Duke said:

"One thing I would like to know, Hibbert—and you might be able to find out from some of the older servants—is why the Earl of Dorset, who was pursuing Miss Claribel a short time ago, cried off and became engaged to somebody else."

"I'll do my best, Your Grace," Hibbert replied, "but the older servants are very closed towards those of us visitors. In fact—what's never happened before in any house we've visited—we eats in a room on our own."

The Duke raised his eye-brows.

He was well aware of the hierarchy in the aristocratic mansions in which there was a protocol below-stairs which was stricter even than that observed in the Dining-Room.

He knew it was usual for Hibbert, being the valet of a Duke, to sit on the Housekeeper's right, unless there were servants of Royalty present.

Following the same tradition, the lady's-maid to his wife, when he had one, would sit on the Butler's right.

Every servant took on the rank of his Master or Mistress, and he knew that at Alverstode there would be no deviation from this rule, although to make it more interesting for his guests he often changed their places at meals so that they would have different people with whom to talk.

"That is certainly strange, Hibbert!" he remarked aloud. "Nevertheless, see what you can find out. I have never known you to fail in matters of this sort."

As he spoke, he knew that he put his valet on his mettle, and he was quite confident that some results would be forthcoming before they left early on Monday morning.

He had in fact been on the point of insisting that they should leave on Sunday, but Lucien had pleaded with him to stay three nights at Stamford Towers, saying anxiously:

"It is only fair to Claribel and me that you should take time to consider your judgement."

The Duke had laughed.

"You make me sound like a Hanging Judge."

"That is what you will be if you do not allow me to marry Claribel," Lucien had replied hotly.

The Duke thought apprehensively that he would undoubtedly have a great deal of trouble with Lucien when he informed his Ward that he would rather see him dead than married to any child of Sir Jarvis Stamford.

As he came in from riding and went into the Breakfast-Room, he found himself wondering what Gióna had had to eat.

He also found it hard when Claribel appeared later in the morning in a ravishing and extremely costly creation not to compare it with Gióna's cheap grey cotton gown and worn slippers.

It would have been impossible for Claribel to live in the same house and not know how her cousin was being treated, and he thought that her dewy-eyed, spring-like appearance was a very clever impersonation of what people would expect her to be like, and not what she really was.

Sir Jarvis had been so determined that the Duke should enjoy his visit to Stamford Towers that every moment of the day had been carefully planned.

The ladies did not rise early, but for the gentlemen after breakfast there was an interesting Mill between two local pugilists who the Duke found were unexpectedly fine exponents of the sport he himself enjoyed.

Before luncheon when the ladies joined them they inspected the stables, and any lover of horse-flesh would have been impressed by Sir Jarvis's Stud.

"I have two horses with which I hope to challenge you next year," Sir Jarvis said complacently to the Duke. "Perhaps together we should challenge the rest of the world and take each prize without having to divide it."

Sir Jarvis spoke with an eagerness which showed the Duke that he was thinking that by next year Claribel and the Viscount would be married.

"It is certainly an idea," the Duke managed to say with a smile, then he changed the subject by admiring the points of a horse they were examining.

After luncheon, at which they were joined by a number of neighbours, there was a Steeple-Chase on Sir Jarvis's private Race-Course which was situated a short distance from the house.

They drove there in Phaetons and brakes, the ladies in their flowered muslins and pretty bonnets holding sunshades over their heads and looking elegant enough for the Royal Enclosure at Ascot.

There was a book-maker to take the gentlemen's bets, not a professional but one of Sir Jarvis's employees, and any profits, they were told, would be shared out at the end of the day amongst the backers.

As this was such an amusing idea the bets were high, although the horses taking part in the Steeple-Chase were so superlative that the Duke acknowledged it was difficult to pick a winner.

It was in fact an entertainment he would have enjoyed if he had not found himself disliking his host more every minute as the day passed and being critical of everything he said, suspecting it to be an untruth.

However, there was nothing untrue about the preparations that were being made for the Ball that was to take place that evening.

The garden was decorated with Chinese lanterns, fairy-lights glittered amongst the flowers and round the edges of the paths, and an Orchestra had been ordered from London which the Duke was aware was the favourite amongst the young women who danced to it every night.

"You must be enjoying yourself, Cousin Valerian," Lucien said to the Duke as they went upstairs to dress for dinner.

"Naturally," the Duke replied.

Lucien followed him into his bedroom and as Hibbert tactfully withdrew he said:

"I suppose it is too soon to ask you if you have made up your mind?"

"About your marriage?"

"I would like to propose to Claribel tonight in the garden."

"If I allowed you to do so," the Duke said loftily, "I think it would be somewhat banal."

"Banal? What do you mean—banal?" Lucien asked testily.

"It is all too obvious, my dear boy; the stars, the moon and the music in the background might all be a stage-set."

"What is wrong with that?"

"If I were going to propose marriage," the Duke replied, "or when I do, I would like it to be in such original circumstances that we would remember it for the rest of our lives."

There was silence. Then Lucien said:

"I see what you mean."

"I have always thought that you would wish to excel in some particular way of your own," the Duke went on, "and I can imagine nothing more important than the moment when you ask a woman to live with you for the rest of your life. It is then that you should show your originality and of course your intelligence."

As he spoke he feared he was rather overdoing the
flattery, but to his relief Lucien accepted the idea and
was smiling as he said:

"You are quite right, Cousin Valerian, I have never
thought of it like that before. Claribel and I have been
to innumerable dances and in a way they are all very
much the same."

"I have always found that," the Duke agreed.

"Then are you saying that if I can think of some really
original way in which I can ask Claribel to be my wife
you will give me your blessing?"

"I am saying nothing of the sort!" the Duke answered
quickly. "I am merely saying that tonight is too soon
and too obvious, and I would like to get to know
Claribel a little better before I consider she is really
good enough for you."

"Good enough for me?" the Viscount echoed in astonishment. "But she is the most beautiful girl in London!"

"And you in a great many people's estimation are the
most handsome and certainly the best-dressed young
man!"

The Duke was not looking at his Ward as he spoke,
but he was aware that he was preening himself.

He thought it a mistake to "over-egg the pudding"
and added quickly:

"As it will undoubtedly take time to tie your cravat to
perfection, I suggest you go and dress. You must not be
late for dinner."

The Viscount gave a little exclamation of horror and
hurried from the room.

The Duke was smiling as Hibbert came back to help
him out of his Hessian boots.

Only when he had bathed and was nearly dressed did
he ask:

"Any news for me, Hibbert?"

"Nothing concrete, Your Grace, just a conversation I
overheard between one of the men who had come in
from the village to help."

"Whom was he speaking to?"

"A footman who's been here for several years and is older than the others."

"What did they say?"

"They didn't know, Your Grace, that I was listening, but Your Grace's aware I've got sharp ears."

The Duke nodded, and Hibbert went on:

"The man from the village said: 'Oi hears we be a-havin' a wedding 'ere soon, Oi shall look for'ard ter that. There'll be a feast an' fireworks, no doubt.'

"'No doubt,' the footman agreed. 'But we was a-countin' on it a month or so ago.'

"'Oi knows that! What happened?'

"'None o' your business!'

"'They says down at th' *Dog and Duck* Jack had stuck 'is oar in.'

"'Whether he did or whether he didn't,' the footman replied, 'an' keep yer mouth shut or you'll be in trouble.'"

Hibbert gave a very good impersonation of the country accent of the man from the village, then said simply:

"That was all, Your Grace."

"Have you any idea who this man Jack is?"

"Not at the moment, Your Grace."

"Try to find out."

"I'll do that, Your Grace."

No more was said, and the Duke went downstairs and found, as he had expected, that the largest Drawing-Room in the house where they were gathering before dinner was packed with people.

He thought with a slight smile that the Viscount outvied every other gentleman present, just as Claribel stood out amongst the younger women like an orchid in a field of buttercups.

The Duke's partners at dinner were sophisticated beauties whom he had met in London and who he learnt were staying at neighbouring houses.

"We were told," one of them said, "that the party

was being given specially for you. I could hardly believe it until I arrived here. I thought you never stayed away except with your own particular friends."

"There are exceptions to every rule," the Duke replied.

"You certainly have a good excuse," the speaker went on.

She was looking at Claribel as she spoke, and added:

"Surely it is unnecessary for her to be so rich, especially when your Ward is a wealthy young man?"

"I have never met anybody yet who had enough money!" the Duke remarked cynically.

The food, if possible, was even better than the night before.

Once again the gentlemen were not allowed to linger over their port but repaired to the Ball-Room.

The Duke had no wish tonight to stay any longer than necessary.

He found himself looking forward to the moment when he could escape and see Giōna.

At the same time, he was aware that to disappear too obviously would be a mistake which might have far-reaching consequences.

He was therefore forced to dance, which was something he most disliked and usually avoided, with several of the older women present, and finally he asked Claribel if she would honour him by being his partner in a waltz.

He noticed that she accepted eagerly. She did not seem shy and was undoubtedly a good dancer.

Only when they had circled the room in silence did she say in an engagingly soft voice:

"I do hope Your Grace is enjoying yourself. Papa has tried so hard to please you, and so have I."

"I should be very ungracious if I did not appreciate your efforts," the Duke answered.

"And we appreciate you," Claribel said.

She spoke in a sweet, ingenuous way which would

have deceived even a more experienced man as being completely natural.

"Lucien was afraid that you might be upset at leaving London in the middle of the Season," the Duke remarked.

"How can he be so foolish?" Claribel replied. "I love the country! It is so beautiful, and when I return home here I have time to think."

"Is that what you want to do?"

"But of course! But knowing how clever Your Grace is, I am afraid you will find I am very ignorant even after an extensive education in many subjects of interest."

It was all too glib, too contrived, the Duke thought, and it had certainly been thought out very carefully, doubtless by Sir Jarvis.

He made the appropriate reply and after the dance was finished he danced with an older woman, then took her through the open windows of the Ball-Room into the garden.

As he did so, he was well aware that Sir Jarvis was watching him go, and he thought that this was the moment when he might escape if he could do it cleverly.

A large number of men who disliked dancing, as the Duke did normally, were standing about under the trees where there was a table containing drinks of every sort, which were also obtainable in the room next to the Ball-Room.

Because it was a warm night most people preferred to be out-of-doors, and as the Duke emerged with his partner on his arm he walked up to two men he knew well.

"Hello, Dawlish!" he said to the man nearest to him. "Would you be so obliging as to fetch my partner and me a glass of champagne? We have both pleased our host by dancing to his Orchestra on an overcrowded floor, and we certainly deserve some refreshment."

Lord Dawlish laughed.

"I was surprised to see you dancing, Alverstode," he said. "I thought you never took to the floor."

"Shall I say that Lady Mary tempted me?" the Duke replied. "I think you all know one another."

They did, and Lady Mary, who was very conscious of her charm, exerted it to keep the three gentlemen amused.

It was only after a little time that the Duke said:

"Excuse me for a moment. There is somebody over there to whom I must speak."

"A man or a woman?" Lady Mary questioned.

"Definitely a man, and definitely about a horse!" the Duke replied, and they all laughed.

He moved away from them and vanished into the shadows, then he was hurrying across the unlit part of the garden which led him to the cascade.

He found the steps, and because he knew how late it was he almost ran through the wood.

The stars and the moon, which was high in the Heavens, made the view that he had seen last night in the sunset even more breathtaking tonight.

But the Duke had eyes only for the fallen tree-trunk a little to his right, and it was with an inexpressible relief that he saw that Giōna was there waiting for him.

"Good-evening!" he said as he sat down beside her. "It was difficult for me to get away."

"I knew it would be, and I did not really expect you would come," she replied. "Besides, I was quite certain you were only a . . . dream."

"I promised you I am very real, and I have been thinking about you," the Duke replied.

He saw her eyes widen in the light from the moon. Her face seemed very pale, and he thought she looked thinner than she had looked the night before.

"Have you had anything to eat all day?" he asked.

She gave a little laugh.

"How can you remember things like that? As a

matter of fact, everybody forgot me as they had so much to do."

The Duke took something from the tails of his evening-coat.

"I thought that might be the case," he said, "so I brought you this."

As he spoke he put down on her knee one of his fine linen handkerchiefs, in which were wrapped a number of finely cut pâté sandwiches."

During the dances he had managed to find them in one of the Sitting-Out Rooms which for the moment was empty, and had quickly transferred the whole plateful into his handkerchief.

Giōna looked at them. Then she asked:

"They are pâté?"

"Yes."

"How can you think of anything so . . . wonderful? I have almost forgotten what it tastes like, except sometimes in the night I pretend I am eating it again. It would be very much more delicious than the thick slabs of cold mutton which appear to be the staple diet in the Servants' Hall."

"I thought the sandwiches would please you," the Duke said.

Giōna wrapped them up again in his handkerchief and said:

"I am not going to eat them now because I want to concentrate on every mouthful, which I cannot do if you are beside me."

"Now this is what I came to tell you," the Duke said. "I am leaving first thing on Monday morning at about eight-thirty, with the excuse that I am in a hurry to get to London."

Giōna stiffened as if she thought that after this she would never see him again, but he went on:

"And you are coming with me!"

"Y-you . . . mean . . . that?"

"All we have to decide is where I pick you up."

Giōna thought for a moment. Then she said:

"There is a thick belt of trees about two or three hundred yards from the Main Lodge. They are enclosed by a fence which is easy to climb."

"You will be there?"

"If you really . . . mean you will . . . take me with . . . you."

"You know I never break my promises."

"I shall be . . . able to bring . . . very little with me."

"There is not need for you to bring anything," the Duke said. "Besides, it might make anyone suspicious who saw you leaving the house carrying a bundle."

"I thought that myself."

"Then just saunter away as if you were going for a walk, and leave me to do everything else."

Giōna clasped her hands together..

"I am . . . dreaming! I know . . . I am . . . dreaming!"

"You are awake," the Duke said firmly, "and you have to use all your intelligence to make sure that nothing stops you from reaching the trees you have described to me."

"I shall . . . never be able to . . . thank you."

"There is no time for that now. I think it would be a mistake, even though I would like to see you again, for me to come here again tomorrow evening."

Giōna nodded.

Her face was turned to his and the Duke saw that now she was looking at him with an expression of trust and something akin to adoration, which he found very touching.

"Keep out of Sir Jarvis's way tomorrow," he said, "and remember that the darkest hour is always before the dawn."

"Nor nearly as . . . dark as it . . . was," Giōna said. "Ever since we met last night there has been a . . . hope in my heart that seemed to . . . come to me from the . . . stars."

"Go on believing and thinking that until Monday morning," the Duke said. "Now I must leave you."

"Yes . . . of course."

"Your back is better?"

"Much . . . much better!" she answered, but he knew she was being brave.

He put out his hand, took hers, and raised it to his lips.

"Until Monday morning," he said, "And come hell or high water I will be waiting for you!"

She gave a little laugh as if she appreciated the expression. Then as the Duke rose to leave he asked:

"By the way, there is somebody employed at the house, or perhaps outside, who is called 'Jack.' Who is he?"

The Duke knew by the way Giōna started that his question surprised her.

"Why do you wish to know?" she asked.

"Is there any reason why you cannot tell me who he is?"

"N-no . . . I suppose . . . not."

The Duke waited and after a moment Giōna said:

"I think you must be speaking of Jack Huntsman."

"What does he do? Is he an employee of Sir Jarvis?"

"He schools the horses . . . and trains those bred on the Estate."

"Anything else?"

"I think you should . . . ask somebody else . . . about him."

"I am asking you, and it might arouse suspicion if Sir Jarvis thought I am inquisitive about any of his staff or about anybody here."

As he spoke, the Duke thought that he was taking a rather unfair advantage. At the same time, here was obviously another mystery, and the sooner he solved it the better.

Giōna was aware of the implications of what he

said, and after a startled little glance at him she said:
"He . . . he gives . . . Claribel . . . riding-lessons."

"Thank you."

The Duke had learnt what he wished to know and thought it was something he might have suspected.

Giōna had risen to stand beside him and he thought in the moonlight how very slim and insubstantial she looked, and in her grey gown she appeared to be part of the shadows.

There was only the light in her eyes to reassure him that she was not just a shadow.

"Good-night, Giōna!" he said in his deep voice. "Take care of yourself until Monday. We have a long drive in front of us, and I would not have you fainting on my hands."

"I would not do that," Giōna replied, "and thank you for the sandwiches."

"I hope you will have more than sandwiches to thank me for in a few days' time."

Then he was hurrying away through the trees, and only when he was out of sight and she could no longer hear his footsteps did Giōna sit down on the trunk of the tree again.

She looked for along time over the moonlit valley beneath her as she prayed that what the Duke had planned would come true.

* * *

Nobody rose early the following morning because the dance had not finished until dawn came up over the horizon and the stars faded in the sky.

The Duke went riding an hour later than usual, but even so he awoke at his usual time and once again was beset by the problems of Giōna, Sir Jarvis, and Lucien, who appeared every moment to the becoming more entangled with Claribel.

However, nobody was aware that he was anything but at his ease as he joined the gentlemen at breakfast.

Experience the World of Barbara Cartland Fragrances

Awaken the romantic in your soul. With the mysteriously beautiful perfumes of romance inspired by Barbara Cartland. There's a heady floral bouquet called *The Heart Triumphant,* an exotic Oriental essence named *Moments of Love* and *Love Wins,* a tantalizing woodsy floral. Each of the three, blended with the poetry and promise of love. For every woman who has ever yearned to love. Yesterday, today and especially tomorrow!

Available at fragrance counters everywhere.

Helena Rubinstein®

Introducing the Romantic World of Barbara Cartland Fragrances

A world of rare and exotic perfumes…
Inspired by the intensely romantic raptures
of love in every Barbara Cartland novel.

Quite a number of them were drinking brandy instead of eating the food which was waiting on a side-table in silver entree dishes kept hot by lighted candles beneath them.

"You look disgustingly healthy, Alverstode!" one of his friends remarked as he sat down at the table.

"You should not drink so much," the Duke replied. "You know as well as I do that one pays for every glass the following morning."

"I know that!" his friend groaned. "But I find it impossible to keep awake without it."

The Duke ate an excellent breakfast, drank with it his usual two cups of coffee, then left the room to find out if the newspapers had been delivered.

The Butler in the Hall informed him that today's and yesterday's newspapers were in the Library, and the Duke found not only the papers but to his satisfaction that there was nobody to disturb him.

He therefore settled down to read the Parliamentary Reports and the Racing News. He had nearly finished the latter when Sir Jarvis came into the room.

"I heard you were here," he said, "and I have come to tell you that we are going down to the stables where one of my men is breaking in a new stallion, a superlative animal which I think might interest you."

The Duke knew he would indeed be most interested and followed Sir Jarvis without asking any questions.

When they reached the paddock which lay beyond the stables he heard Sir Jarvis say to the man who was waiting for them:

"Bring out Rufus, Jack, and let us see how you handle him."

The Duke had heard exactly what he had hoped for and expected, and he was more interested in the man who was handling the horse than in the horse itself.

Jack Huntsman, who was over thirty, he thought, was a good-looking, somewhat raffish man with an insolent air which would undoubtedly gain him a lot of success with women.

His physique was almost perfect, slim, broad-shouldered, and while definitely not a gentleman he was a cut above the grooms who worked in the stables.

Rufus was spirited, obstreperous, and determined to unseat the man on his back, but there was no doubt that Huntsman was a good rider and an experienced one.

However, the Duke thought he was a little more severe with the spur and the whip than was necessary for such a young animal.

They watched for about twenty minutes until Sir Jarvis, as if he thought the Duke might be bored, said:

"I have several other horses for you to see which were out to grass yesterday, but I have had them brought in for you to have a look at them."

"I have a feeling you are trying to make me jealous," the Duke said.

"On the contrary, I am still interested in the idea of a certain co-operation between us."

The Duke wondered what Sir Jarvis would say if he replied that he would rather co-operate with the devil.

Instead he merely answered enigmatically:

"I am always interested in new ideas."

Then he changed the subject by asking Sir Jarvis what horse he was entering for the races at Ascot.

To the Duke the day seemed interminable, the hours passing slowly while he was well aware that Lucien was becoming every moment more closely involved with Claribel.

They sat together, talked together, and in the afternoon they went driving in one of Sir Jarvis's High-Perched Phaetons.

At dinner the Viscount was naturally placed on Claribel's right, and she made no effort to speak to the man on her other side.

After dinner several of the guests wandered outside

onto the terrace, but the Duke settled himself at the card-table and played for high stakes until one of his opponents threw down his cards, saying as he did so:

"You are too damned lucky, Alverstode, and I am too damned sleepy. I am going to bed."

"And so am I," the Duke's partner said. "I am getting too old for late nights."

He was not the only one, while the ladies definitely were not looking as beautiful as they had the night before and were all ready to proceed up the stairs, most of them carrying lighted candles in gold stands.

Hibbert was waiting in the Duke's bedroom, but when he went to take off his evening-coat the Duke held up his hand.

"What I want you to do, Hibbert," he said in a low voice, "is to find out how I can reach the stables without being seen. How can I manage it?"

"Is it something I can do for Your Grace?" Hibbert asked.

"No, I want to go myself."

"Best wait a little while, Your Grace."

"I agree," the Duke said, "but not too long."

Hibbert left him to come back about ten minutes later.

There was no need for either of them to speak. The Duke merely followed Hibbert along the main corridor, where half the lights had already been extinguished, and down a narrow staircase to the ground floor.

They moved through twisting passages until they reached a door which Hibbert unbolted and unlocked to let the Duke out.

"You'll be able to find you way back, Your Grace?" he whispered.

The Duke thought that if he could find his way about Portugal and France with the hopelessly inadequate maps which the troops had been issued, he could find his way back to his bedroom at Stamford Towers.

Outside, he took his bearings and set off in the direction of the stables.

He had noticed this morning that there was a large Barn filled with hay set rather picturesquely amongst some birch trees.

It did not appear to be in use, or perhaps the hay was just in reserve for an emergency, but it struck the Duke that it would be a very romantic place for a rendezvous near the house.

He moved towards it, keeping in the shadows until he finally found a place where he could hide behind some rhododendron bushes.

Then he settled himself comfortably, aware that if he was wrong in his supposition he would have a long wait and what would prove to be a pointless waste of time.

And yet his instinct that had never failed him told him unmistakably that he was on the right track, and as usual his instinct was right.

After he had been waiting for about a quarter-of-an-hour there was a sound from the direction of the house and from another door came a figure in a dark blue velvet cloak over a white evening-gown.

Claribel, for that was who the Duke knew it was, kept close to a hedge of flowering fuchsias which was overshadowed by chestnut trees.

When she had nearly reached the Barn, the Duke was aware that somebody had come out of the darkness of it and was waiting for her.

One quick glance told him that it was Jack Huntsman, and he waited only a few more seconds to see them disappear.

Then hurriedly but silently he retraced his steps back to the house, along the passages, and up the stairs to the main corridor where his own bedroom was situated.

He did not stop there, however, but hurried on for quite a long way until he reached the room where he knew Lucien was sleeping.

Just for a moment he hesitated, wondering whether he was doing the right thing.

Disillusionment was, as the Duke knew personally, something that could be very painful and leave a scar for a long time.

And yet the alternative was worse: to be married to a woman who was promiscuous and who would swear eternal fidelity while she was still enamoured with another man.

The Duke's lips were set in a hard line as he opened the bedroom door without knocking.

* * *

Lucien had not felt tired when he went to bed. He had been too elated at the things Claribel had said to him.

"Think how wonderful it will be when we are married," she had said in her soft, beguiling voice. "We can give even bigger and better parties than Papa gave last night."

"I am not interested in parties," Lucien said, "only in being with you."

"We shall be together," Claribel said, "but it will be exciting to entertain and to stay with your Guardian."

"I want to show you Alverstode," Lucien said, "but what is more important to me is Frome House. It is not so big or perhaps so magnificent, but it is beautiful, and when my mother was alive everybody said that the parties at Frome were more amusing than those they enjoyed anywhere else."

"Did you entertain Royalty?" Claribel asked.

"Royalty is usually rather boring because there is so much pomp and circumstance involved."

"Nevertheless, that is what I would enjoy," she said, "and you will arrange it for me, will you not?"

"You know I will do anything that you want," Lucien replied passionately. "Tell me that you love me and that no other man has ever mattered to you in the same way."

"You know that I love you," Claribel said, "but you must not be jealous."

"I am jealous!" Lucien insisted. "I hate your dancing with anybody but me. I hate the way men look at you, and if a man flirts with you when we are married I swear I will kill him!"

Claribel gave a very pretty laugh.

"Oh, dearest, there is no need for such dramatics. Once we are married, I will be your wife."

"The most beautiful, adorable, exciting wife any man ever had," Lucien said.

She had put her hand on his and he thought it would be impossible to feel so intensely without dying of the wonder of it.

When he reached his room he had pulled off his evening-coat and settled down to write a poem to Claribel.

He thought he would tell the servants to see that it was put on her breakfast-tray tomorrow morning, and he could imagine how lovely she would look as she read it.

However, he found it a little harder than he had expected, and he had written only two lines to his satisfaction when the door opened and he saw to his surprise the Duke.

He put down the quill-pen, wondering as he did so what his Guardian could have to say to him.

He was surprised when the Duke shut the door very quietly behind him and crossed the room to say in a lowered voice:

"I want you to come with me, Lucien, I have something to show you."

"At this time of the night?"

"I know it is late, but it is important."

"Of course I will do what you want," Lucien said, "but I cannot imagine . . ."

"Let us hurry," the Duke said, "and I want you to

promise me that from the moment we leave this room you will not speak a word."

"But why?"

"Just give me your promise."

"Of course, if you want me to, but I would like to understand . . ."

"There is no time for explanations," the Duke said quickly. "Come with me, and whatever happens, whatever occurs, I hold you to your promise that you will say and do nothing."

The Viscount smiled.

"This is all very 'cloak and dagger'!"

All the same, he was beginning to be intrigued.

He put on his evening-coat again as he spoke, and the Duke opened the door ad led the way down the corridor.

Once again he traversed the staircase and the corridors and they went out through the door he had left standing open.

Only when Lucien had followed him behind the rhododendron bushes did the Duke become aware that the moon was now high in the sky directly overhead and the Barn was as brilliantly illuminated as it would be by daylight.

The Viscount was looking about him in sheer astonishment.

He could not see why his Guardian had brought him here in the middle or the night, for no apparent reason, and he wondered if in fact the Duke had been overimbibing at dinner.

Then he told himself that that was extremely unlikely and there must be a good reason, but what it could be he had not the slightest idea.

In the meantime, as he was obviously supposed to wait, he might as well finish his poem in his head, which would enable him to write it down as soon as he was permitted to return to his own room.

By the time he had added three more lines to those he had already composed, he was feeling rather stiff from standing for so long.

Then he was suddenly aware that the Duke stiffened.

He looked at him, then followed the direction of his eyes, and froze into immobility.

Coming from the direction of the Barn, which was almost directly opposite him, two people appeared.

It was Claribel's deep blue cloak that Lucien noticed first, for it was one he had helped her into earlier in the evening when they had walked in the garden and she had said she was feeling the cold.

He had placed it lingeringly over her shoulders and she had thanked him in a way which made him long frantically to kiss her, but he realised there were too many people about.

Now he could see her talking to some man whom he did not recognise, and he was sure it was nobody from the house-party.

Claribel took a step forward and Lucien could see now to his surprise that the man was wearing riding-clothes.

Then as he could only wonder why Claribel was there and what she was doing, she turned back to the man and put her arms round his neck.

He pulled her roughly to him. Then he was kissing her, a long passionate kiss which made the Viscount feel as if a red-hot poker were searing his forehead.

As he realised fully what was happening, he would have rushed forward, but the Duke, anticipating this action, took his wrist in a grip of iron.

As he did so, Lucien remembered that he had given his word that whatever happened he would not speak or move.

He thought afterwards that it might have been for a few minutes or a few hours that he watched the woman he loved locked in another man's arms.

Then they separated and Claribel turned and ran

swiftly back along the side of the fuchsia bushes in the shadow of the chestnut trees and disappeared.

Jack Huntsman yawned before he walked not into the Barn but towards the stables.

Only when he was out of sight did the Duke relinquish his hold on his Ward's wrist and lead the way back into the house.

Chapter Four

Neither the Duke nor the Viscount spoke until they had reached the latter's bedroom.

Then Lucien stalked in to say:

"I am leaving!"

His voice was raw and the Duke was aware how much he was suffering.

"I think that would be a mistake," he said quietly.

"If you think I am going to stay here and meet that woman again, you are much mistaken! She lied to me, she pretended, and all the time . . ."

Words failed the Viscount and he clenched his fingers together in an effort at self-control, but his voice broke on the last word.

"What would be a mistake," the Duke said, "is for them to have the slightest idea of your feelings or of what you have discovered."

"I want to confront them with it!" the Viscount muttered between gritted teeth.

"I am sure you do, and it is what I would like to do myself," the Duke said. "But you will have your revenge, that I can assure you, though not yet!"

He realised that the Viscount was hardly attending to him and after a moment he went on:

"What I suggest we do is leave with dignity, without either Sir Jarvis or his daughter having any idea of what we have discovered, and I would be obliged if you would drive my Phaeton to London."

For a moment what the Duke had said hardly percolated the Viscount's dazed mind. Then he asked in an almost incredulous tone:

"Did you say—drive your Phaeton?"

"That is what I asked you to do."

"But you never allow anybody to drive your horses!"

"On this occasion it is important that you should do so. I have sent for my D'Orsay Curricle as I have a call to make in another part of the country before I return to London."

The only thing that could have soothed the Viscount's feelings at this particular moment was the prospect of driving the Duke's outstanding team of chestnuts which was the envy of every owner of horse-flesh.

It was also well known that he allowed nobody other than himself to drive either them or a number of other horses in his possession which he looked on as being particularly outstanding.

Realising he had captured his Ward's attention, the Duke went on:

"We depart at eight-thirty and Hibbert will call you at seven o'clock. We will leave our host believing that the visit has been a success, and only when you do not communicate with his daughter will he begin to worry, and so will she, as to what has occurred."

As if he thought this would certainly perturb Claribel, the Viscount's eyes sharpened and the Duke was aware that he was now thirsting for revenge.

"Let me assure you," he said, "that I have a debt almost as great as yours to settle with Sir Jarvis, and I am just waiting for details which will confound and, I hope, destroy him!"

"Do you really mean that?"

"I am not speaking lightly."

"Then tell me what you intend to do."

"All in good time," the Duke replied, "and when you

do hear it you will realise, although you must find it difficult at this moment, that you have had a lucky escape."

He did not say any more.

He only opened the door, nodded to his Ward, and left him to what he knew would be the misery and despair of any young man who was in love and realises he has been betrayed.

Then when he reached his own bedroom the Duke was thinking of Gīōna and hoping with a fervency that surprised him that nothing would prevent her from reaching the wood where he was to meet her the next morning.

* * *

Driving across country in a D'Orsay Curricle which travelled faster than any other vehicle the Duke possessed, and which was drawn by his most reliable pair of perfectly matched black stallions, he thought that everything had gone more smoothly than he had dared anticipate.

When he and Lucien had breakfasted downstairs at eight o'clock there had been nobody to keep them company, and only when they had left the Breakfast-Room and were proceeding across the Hall did Sir Jarvis come hurrying down the staircase.

"I had no idea," he exclaimed before he had reached the last step, "that you were leaving so early! I cannot imagine why I was not informed."

"I understood you were aware," the Duke answered, "that I have to reach London as early as possible. You know as well as I do that His Royal Highness dislikes being kept waiting."

There was nothing Sir Jarvis could say to this, and he turned to the Viscount to ask:

"Why must you go too, Frome? I know that Claribel was expecting you to stay for luncheon."

The Duke was aware that his Ward had stiffened as

Sir Jarvis spoke to him, and, being afraid of what he might say, he interposed:

"Lucien is obliging me by driving my Phaeton," he said. "Another reason why I have to leave so early is that I have to call on my way on an elderly relative who is in ill health. It is a bore, but a duty which cannot be avoided."

"I quite understand," Sir Jarvis said in a voice which showed he did nothing of the sort.

He was in fact looking at both of his guests with an expression which told the Duke very clearly that he was perturbed at their precipitate departure.

What was more disturbing was that the Viscount had not formally asked him for his daughter's hand in marriage.

"A most enjoyable visit!" the Duke said as he moved towards the front door. "Once again, I must congratulate you both on your house and the beauties of your garden."

Sir Jarvis did not answer because he was walking behind the Duke, beside Lucien.

"Claribel will be disappointed that you are returning to London so soon," he said, "but I hope you will be able to dine with us tomorrow. We shall look forward to seeing you."

The Viscount was about to refuse, when the Duke turned his head slightly and he changed what he was about to say to mutter:

"You are very kind."

Then before Sir Jarvis could say any more he had swung himself up into the Duke's Phaeton to take up the reins with an undisguised eagerness.

The Duke just paused to mutter to his Head Groom:

"Be careful His Lordship does not spring them, Ben!"

Then he walked a few paces to his D'Orsay Curricle, and his second groom, handing over the reins, sprang up into the small seat behind.

The black stallions were fresh and hard to control, but the Duke had time to notice that Sir Jarvis, standing on the steps and watching them go, had a puzzled expression on his face and a frown between his eyes.

The Duke followed the Phaeton ahead of him until as they passed through the large ornamental gates he noted with satisfaction that the dusty road outside was empty and there were no houses in sight.

It was quite easy to see where the high wall of the Estate ended and the wooden fence which bordered the wood began. He drew his horses slowly to a standstill, saying to his groom as he did so:

"Put up the hood, Ben."

He thought the groom might be surprised, for it was well-known among his staff that unless it was raining torrentially or snowing His Grace preferred driving in the open.

His groom clambered down to pull up the half-hood which was skilfully designed so as to cause the least possible reduction of speed, and the Duke saw a slight figure climb lithely over the wooden fence which enclosed the trees and come running over the rough grass towards him.

He wasted no time in words but merely put out his hand to draw her into the seat beside him, then drove on, hardly giving Ben time to scramble up behind.

They proceeded for a little while in silence, the Duke well aware that Giōna was breathless not so much from the quickness with which she had run to him as from excitement.

He glanced at her and saw that her eyes were shining and there was a faint flush on her pale cheeks.

He also realised, now that he could see her in the daylight, that she was painfully thin, and the bones of her wrists were protruding in the same manner that he had noticed amongst the children in Portugal after the French had retreated, taking all the available food with them.

She was still wearing the same grey gown that he had seen her wearing before, only now there was a small woolen shawl over her shoulders.

He thought it was sensible of her to protect herself against feeling cold during the long journey that lay ahead of them.

She wore no bonnet, and for the first time he could see the colour of her hair. It was not dark as he had expected but was the colour, he thought which one could most nearly describe as ash, but which was very much more beautiful than the mere word suggested.

It seemed to hold both the light and the darkness in it, as if sunshine and shadow combined to make a colour he had never seen on any other woman.

It was the perfect complement to her eyes, which were the grey of a pigeon's feathers.

"You have escaped!" he said with a smile.

"I cannot... believe it! Am I really... leaving all that... despair and... misery behind?"

"I swear that nobody shall ever beat you again," the Duke said, "and the future I envisage for you will, I believe, make up for the past."

"How can I have been so... fortunate as to be in that one... special place when you came through the... wood to look at the... view?"

"Being a Greek, you must be aware that the gods look after their own!" the Duke said lightly.

She gave a little chuckle before she said:

"I am very... very grateful to... them."

After that they drove in silence, the Duke enjoying the perfection of his horses, Giōna aware that every mile took her farther away from the terror of Sir Jarvis.

Only when she saw an Inn ahead and realised that the Duke was slowing did she look at him enquiringly, and as if she had asked the question he said:

"I am quite certain you are hungry and had no breakfast before you left."

"Even if it had been there, I would have been too excited to eat it."

"I have already warned you that I dislike women who faint from exhaustion!"

"I shall be all right."

"I have no wish to take a chance on that."

It was as they drew nearer to the Inn that Giōna said:

"Supposing I am seen? We are not so far from Stamford Towers, and Uncle Jarvis might make enquiries about me."

"I have thought of that," the Duke replied. "This is a very out-of-the-way, old-fashioned Inn where your uncle would never expect me to eat."

He thought that Giōna was still unconvinced, and he added:

"You will find tucked into the side of your seat my evening-cape which will cover your gown, and I am going to suggest, as you look very young and very slight, that if you let your hair down I shall mention quite casually that you are my younger sister who has just left school."

Giōna gave a little laugh of sheer amusement.

"You are . . . wonderful! You make everything so . . . exciting and exactly like a story in a novel."

As she spoke she was pulling the pins from her hair, which was arranged very simply in a large coil at the back of her neck.

As it fell over her shoulders the Duke saw that it was long and he thought that like everything else about her it was very beautiful.

It took Giōna only a moment to slip the woollen shawl from her shoulders and to clasp the Duke's black cape with its velvet collar and crimson silk lining at the base of her throat.

As they drove into the courtyard of the Inn the Duke saw the Inn-Keeper approaching and knew he was delighted at the prospect of guests who owned such superb horses.

Ben, who obviously had his Master's instructions, jumped down to say:

"This be Sir Alexander Albion, who requires a private room where he can have luncheon for himself and his sister Miss Juliet Albion."

The Landlord scratched his head.

"Oi be honoured that the gent'man should patronise moi Inn. Oi've no private Parlour, but there be nobidy in the Dining-Room."

"Then keep it that way," Ben said, and hurried to help Giōna down from the Curricle

While she washed her hands and tidied her hair Giōna explained to the Inn-Keeper's wife that she had lost her bonnet in the wind from the speed at which she and her brother had travelled over the open country.

"Have ye got naught to cover yer head, Miss?" the Inn-Keeper's wife asked solicitously.

"My brother would not stop to fetch my bonnet," she replied, "but he has consented to have the hood up, and I am quite all right."

"Oi might 'ave a piece o' ribbon, Miss, if that'd be any help," the Inn-Keeper's wife suggested.

"That would be very kind of you," Giōna replied.

Accordingly, when she came downstairs with her long hair neatly brushed there was a blue ribbon to keep it in place, and it was tied in a small bow on the top of her head.

There was a twinkle in the Duke's eyes as she explained how she got it, and when they were alone having luncheon he said:

"Now you really do look like a School-girl!"

"In three months' time I shall be nineteen," Giōna replied.

Before this she had exclaimed with delight when they

sat down in the small Dining-Room of the Inn to be served first with slices of pâté.

"How can they have anything like this here?" she began.

Then she added quickly:

"But of course, you brought it with you."

"My valet is very solicitous for my comfort," the Duke answered. "He does not approve of the type of food which is obtainable in most country Inns."

"I am glad I am so hungry!" Giōna said with a smile.

But although the cold chicken stuffed with grapes and mushrooms was undoubtedly delicious, she could eat only a very little of it, and the Duke was aware that after the privation she had endured it would take her some time to regain a normal appetite.

The wine which Hibbert had also provided from Sir Jarvis's cellar tasted as golden as it looked, and Giōna said with a little sigh as the meal finished:

"I have lain awake at night thinking of food like this, but I thought I should never taste it again."

"I shall look forward to seeing you do better justice to it in future," the Duke said drily.

Then, as he had expected, Giōna asked:

"Where are you . . . taking me?"

"To somebody who will look after you while I make the enquiries you wish me to make."

Giōna looked a little apprehensive.

"I . . . I shall not be with . . . you?"

"Not at the moment, and I think you are intelligent enough to be aware that as you are under-age and your uncle is your Guardian, I could be accused of abducting a minor."

Giōna gave a little cry of horror and said:

"I had forgotten . . . forgive me . . . but I had forgotten there was a law to that effect in England . . . I should not have . . . come with you."

"Would you have been able to refuse my offer of help?" the Duke asked.

"B-but the punishment for . . . abduction is . . . I believe . . . transportation."

"You have not answered my question."

"If I tell you I would have refused, it would not be . . . true," Giōna said. "You are like Perseus saving me from the Sea Monster, or St. Michael and all his angels coming to my aid! But now that I am . . . free I . . . realise I must . . . leave you."

"How do you propose to do that?" the Duke enquired.

"If you give me a little . . . money . . . a very little . . . I could somehow find my way to the village where Mama lived before she ran away with Papa. My grandfather will now be dead . . . but there are people who will remember him . . . and who might find me a way of earning my own living."

The Duke, looking at her closely, was aware that she was not speaking for effect but was quite serious in her proposition.

"I have very different plans for you," he said, "and because I think you feel you are under some obligation to me . . ."

"A very big one," Giōna interposed.

"You will do what I want," the Duke finished.

"You know I will do anything . . . anything you ask of me," she promised.

The Duke knew it was in the nature of a vow.

"Very well," he said in a practical tone, "the first thing is to chose a name for you, because naturally you cannot call yourself Stamford."

"N-no . . . of course not!"

"I was going to ask you anyway," the Duke went on, "the name of your mother before she married."

"It was Hamilton."

The Duke repeated it as if he fixed it in his mind. Then he said:

"Because of your Christian name, and because you do not look entirely English, I somehow expected it to be Greek."

Giōna smiled.

"My grandmother was half-Greek. Her name was . . . Andreas."

"Then that is how you shall be called for now," the Duke said. "Giōna Andreas. I hope it pleases you."

"I am very proud of my Greek blood."

"There is a straightness to your nose," the Duke added, "which I have seen on the Caryatid maidens at the Acropolis, and particularly on statues of the Goddess Athene."

"Now you are making me so conceited that I feel I can hold my head high wherever I happen to be in the future."

"I think that is something you have done during the difficulties of the past," the Duke said. "Now I have one more question before we are on our way. Have you any idea of the year in which your mother and father were married?"

"She often said to me that I was born exactly twelve months after she ran away with my father," Giōna said, "so I am sure that she was married in August 1799."

"That makes the marriage much easier to trace than it would have been otherwise."

"Then you . . . really will . . . search for a . . . record of it?"

Giōna's voice was breathless, and the Duke said:

"I think you are almost insulting me by asking the question."

"I know you said you would . . . but I can hardly believe . . . when you are so important and obviously have so many things to occupy your mind . . . that you would really . . . concern yourself with my . . . problems."

"I thought I had convinced you that I am concerned."

"You have now, and I want to say 'thank you' but my vocabulary is very limited . . . so I can only say it from my heart . . . and I hope you understand."

"I will certainly try too."

Because there was something in Giōna's voice that

was very moving, he deliberately replied casually, and as she spoke he rose to his feet.

He was used to women falling in love with him, and although he was quite certain that Giōna did not know the meaning of the word in the sense in which he knew it, the look he had thought of as one of admiration was still there.

He was uncomfortably aware that it would be an additional problem if she regarded him as anything more than a rescuer and a Sword of Justice.

That was what he intended to be, the Duke thought, the avenger of her uncle who had treated her so abominably and who should be punished as he would be prepared to punish anybody he found torturing a child or an animal.

He found it impossible to forget the weals he had seen on Giōna's back.

He was also certain that she was being truthful when she said that Sir Jarvis was prepared to weaken her hold on life by inadequate feeding and by what amounted, apart from her physical suffering, to mental persecution.

The mere fact that he had styled her a "bastard" and had defamed her mother would prey on the mind of any young girl as sensitive as Giōna who suddenly found herself orphaned and bereft of everything that was familiar.

Then, combined with Sir Jarvis's brutality was the perfidy of his daughter, and the more he thought of them both and of their behaviour, the more the Duke was determined that they should pay for their sins.

He knew he had a long way to go before he would have the satisfaction of bringing his plans to success and getting Sir Jarvis where he wanted him—on his knees.

The Duke had learnt when boxing never to underestimate his opponent and during the war to expect the unexpected.

As they drove on he was going over and over in his

mind every detail of what had now become a campaign,
determined to make sure he had not been careless or
left anything to chance.

It was almost as if he were drawing up a battle-plan
and looking for weak spots where the enemy might
break through.

As the afternoon progressed the countryside changed
a little, and as Giōna looked about her with interest,
the Duke knew they were nearing Buckinghamshire,
where the Alverstode Estate was situated.

He now knew every highway and lane, and as if the
horses were aware that they were not far from home
and their own comfortable stable they seemed to quick-
en their pace without waiting for their driver to encourage them.

Twenty minutes later the Duke said in a tone of
satisfaction:

"Welcome, Giōna! We are now driving on land
which has been in my family's hands for four hundred
years."

"How exciting!" Giōna exclaimed. "But I thought
you were not . . . taking me to your house."

"I am taking you to stay with my grandmother," the
Duke answered. "She is a very redoubtable old lady
who was once a great beauty, but now, because she is
old and suffers from rheumatism, she is often very
bored. I have the idea you will give her a new interest."

"Are you going to . . . tell her the whole . . . truth about
me?"

"I shall tell her because she will enjoy it," the Duke
replied, "but nobody else must know except my Ward,
Lucien. You quite understand, Giōna, that nobody,
and I mean nobody, must be taken into your confidence."

"I promise I will speak of it to nobody!" Giōna said.
"But if I am with your grandmother I shall . . . see you
sometimes?"

"I am not yet ready to disappear," the Duke replied briefly.

Once again they drove in silence.

As they drove in through a pair of finely wrought ornamental gates Giōna saw in front of them not a large but a very beautiful house built in the reign of Queen Anne, and the Duke was aware that she clasped her hands together as if she was nervous.

He thought as he glanced at her that he had never known a woman whose eyes were so revealing and showed her innermost feelings as clearly as if he were looking into a clear stream.

There was no time to say anything as he drew his horses up outside the porticoed front door and Ben jumped down to run to the horses' heads.

As he did so, two grooms came running from the stables beside the house, touching their forelocks respectfully when they saw who was in the Chariot.

The servants were slower in opening the front door, and it was the Duke who helped Giōna onto the ground, and as her fingers touched his, he was aware that she was cold and trembling.

"There is nothing to make you afraid," he said quietly as they walked up the steps to the front door.

A Butler with white hair came hurrying into the Hall.

"Your Grace!" he exclaimed. "This is a surprise, and Her Grace'll be delighted. She was complaining only yesterday that your Grace was neglecting her."

"I am here now, Simpson, as you see," the Duke replied. "Where is Her Grace?"

"In her *Boudoir*, Your Grace. Seeing as she's been in some pain these last two days, Her Grace hasn't come downstairs."

"Then I will go up to her," the Duke said, "and I want you, Simpson, to take Miss Andreas to Mrs. Meadows so that she can tidy herself after our long drive."

"I'll do that, Your Grace."

Simpson smiled at Giōna as he said:

"If you'll come with me, Miss, but we'd best walk up the stairs after His Grace, seeing as I can't go as fast as I used to."

The Duke went ahead, aware as he walked along the landing at the top of the stairs that Giōna was talking pleasantly to the old Butler who could only climb up slowly.

The Duke knocked on the door of his grandmother's *Boudoir*, then opened it.

As he had expected, she was seated in an arm-chair in the window with her legs raised on a foot-stool and covered with an ermine rug.

On her lap was a small King Charles spaniel which first growled when the Duke opened the door, then barking with excitement bounded towards him.

The Duke bent to pat the spaniel before he walked towards his grandmother.

He noted that despite the lines of pain on her face she was looking very beautiful, and her white hair was as well arranged as if she were attending an Assembly.

She was also wearing several rows of pearls, rings on her fingers, and a bracelet which glittered in the sunshine as she held out her hands towards him.

"Valerian, is it really you? How delightful to see you!"

"It is really me, Grandmama," the Duke replied, "and forgive me for being so remiss in neglecting you, but the Regent is very demanding."

"He always was, even when he was a young man," the Dowager agreed, "but you did not let me know you were coming."

"I did not know myself until two days ago, Grandmama, and now I need your help."

The Duchess released his hand and said:

"If it is another of those tiresome orphans you wish me to employ, the answer is 'No'! The last one you persuaded me to have in the house upset Simpson with his impertinence, and the one before broke half-a-dozen of my best Sèvres tea-cups."

The Duke had heard all this before, and he was just about to reply when his grandmother went on:

"You have two, or is it three, Orphanages you support, and that is where orphans should be. Not with me!"

The Duke was well aware that it was no use explaining that after a certain age the orphans had to leave the Orphanage to make room for other children and go out to work.

But as he drew up a chair beside his grandmother, he said:

"I have with me, Grandmama, a very different orphan from those you have helped before."

"I will not have him!" the Duchess said firmly. "So before you start trying to coax me, Valerian, the answer is 'No'!"

"I am sorry about that," the Duke said, "because this orphan—who is a 'she,' by the way, and not a 'he'—will intrigue you, and I need your help not only in looking after her but in punishing and bringing to justice a man whose crimes will astound and horrify you."

"I very much doubt it," the Duchess replied.

There was silence. Then, as if her curiosity was too much for her, she asked:

"Who is this man?"

"Sir Jarvis Stamford!"

The Duchess stared at her grandson incredulously. Then she said:

"Not the father of that girl whom Lucien has been pursuing and whom everybody expects him to marry?"

The Duke laughed.

"Grandmama, you are incorrigible! There is not a rumour, a piece of gossip, or a scandal that you, living here in the country, are not aware of long before it reaches me!"

"There is not much else to amuse me now that I can hardly leave my bedroom!" the Duchess snapped.

"I am not complaining," the Duke said. "It only makes my story easier. Yes, Sir Jarvis Stamford is the father of the girl who *did* interest Lucian."

He deliberately accentuated the past tense, and the Duchess sat up in her chair.

"You mean he has finished with her? Or has she refused him? From all I hear, she would be ready to capture somebody more important than Lucien if she could find him."

"What I am going to tell you, Grandmama," the Duke said, "is the whole story from the beginning, and when you have heard it you will understand why nobody must have any idea of the truth, except yourself."

The Duke spoke in a voice which made his grandmother aware that what he had to impart was in fact very serious.

Then before he could speak the door opened and a footman came in carrying a silver tray on which there were two glasses and a wine-cooler containing a bottle of champagne.

He set the tray down on a small table, and when he would have poured out the wine the Duke rose to say:

"I will do that, Henry."

"I thanks Your Grace."

The footman would have withdrawn, but the Duke saw that on the tray there was also a plate of sandwiches.

"Ask Simpson," he said, "to see that Miss Andreas, who is with Mrs. Meadows, has tea and plenty to eat. I am sure Mrs. Goodwin is already cooking some hot scones for tea."

"I'll tell Mr. Simpson, Your Grace."

The door shut and the Duchess said:

"Now, tell me about Sir Jarvis and of course Lucien. I am not accepting this orphan of yours or providing her with hot scones until I know what this is all about."

The Duke handed his grandmother a glass of champagne.

"I know the Doctor has forbidden you any alcohol, Grandmama," he said, "but as you listen to my story you will need some sustenance."

"What you are really saying is that you hope the wine will make me mellow enough to accede to your wishes! I assure you I shall not let it cloud my common sense!"

The Duke smiled slightly, helped himself to a sandwich, and took a sip of champagne before he began.

Then he related exactly what had happened since he had condescended to visit Stamford Towers.

The Duchess did not interrupt. She merely became so interested that she forgot to drink her champagne.

She listened with her eyes on her grandson's face as he told her about the beatings Giōna had received and the moment by the stables when he and Lucien had watched from behind the rhododendron bushes as Claribel kissed her lover good-night.

Only when he had finished did the Duchess exclaim:

"I have always known you to be truthful, at least to me, Valerian, and you could not have invented a plot more incredible than anything fabricated by Sir Walter Scott."

"It sounds fantastic," the Duke agreed, "but I can assure you it is the truth and is very real to Giōna."

"What sort of girl is she?"

"Beautiful, intelligent, and with Greek blood in her veins."

The Duchess raised her eye-brows as she said:

"From what you have just told me, I guess that villain Sir Jarvis told her she was born out of wedlock so as to make sure she did not flaunt the fact that she was his niece."

"That is my explanation," the Duke agreed, "and it is all part of his plan to hide a guilty secret."

"And what is that?"

"That is what I intend to find out," the Duke replied. "He obviously paid his brother to stay abroad, the residue of which he very conveniently claimed when he died. He was also afraid that Giōna might in some way reveal whatever it is that he has been hiding for so long."

He paused before he continued slowly:

"This must be the reason why he has allowed her to meet nobody and why he wishes to dispose of her without actually having to commit murder."

"I never believed such things happened except in books!" the Duchess exclaimed.

"Well, they do!" the Duke replied. "But you will now understand, Grandmama, why I want to leave Giōna with you. I want you to turn her into the attractive young woman she should be, so that when the moment comes it will be impossible for Sir Jarvis, short of shooting her dead, to deny her existence."

"And when will that moment be?"

"When I am ready!" the Duke replied, and there was something ominous in his voice.

* * *

In an attractive bedroom, Giōna, having washed and tidied herself to the best of her ability, waited apprehensively.

An elaborate tea had been brought to her by two footmen, and while she appreciated the hot scones, the paper-thin sandwiches, and the fairy-cakes that were so light it seemed they might fly away, she found that after a few mouthfuls she was not hungry.

She was too afraid of what would happen to her when the Duke left her, as she knew he intended to do.

She found herself wondering frantically if it would not be best after all to go off on her own and hide somewhere where Sir Jarvis could not find her and she would not be an encumbrance or a danger to the Duke.

But she had not a penny-piece in her possession and she certainly had nothing she could sell.

She had been almost too astounded to protest when after Sir Jarvis had brought her home from Italy to Stamford Towers her clothes were taken from her.

Instead she had been provided with the ugly grey cotton gowns that were made by the seamstress in the house.

"Why should I have to dress like this?" she had asked, being able in those days to show some spirit even though she was already aware that her uncle disliked her.

"You will wear what I tell you to!" he replied sharply. "As a bastard whom your father and mother have foisted on the world, you are fortunate I do not send you to the Workhouse or make you an assistant in an Orphanage to look after the unfortunates in the same position as yourself."

"I will not have you telling such lies about my father and mother!" Giōna replied hotly. "They were married... I know they were married! Do you imagine that Mama, who was the daughter of a Parson and believed in God, would ever have done anything so... wicked?"

Sir Jarvis had not argued, he had merely beaten her. Only after innumerable beatings which had left her humiliated and in agonising pain had Giōna realised that there was no use trying to defend her father and mother, who were dead.

Now she thought that when the Duke had gone perhaps his grandmother would despise her and once again she would be little more than a servant in a different household.

The door opened and Giōna thought that Mrs. Meadows, who had left her alone to enjoy her tea, had come to collect the tray, but it was the Duke.

She jumped to her feet with a little cry.

"I was afraid you had... forgotten me!"

"I am sorry if it seemed a long time " he said, "but
my grandmother was very interested in all I had to tell
her, and now I want you to come and meet her."

"I . . . I was thinking that perhaps . . ." Giōna began in
a hesitating little voice.

Because the Duke knew by the expression in her
eyes exactly what she was thinking, he interrupted to
say:

"I told you to trust me. You also promised to do
everything I wanted. I hold you to that promise, Giōna."

She raised her chin and he liked the pride which
made her do so.

She had taken off his elegant evening-cape and he
thought that despite the ugly grey gown she wore, with
her hair falling over her shoulders she looked very
lovely.

At the same time, he was aware that his grandmother
would not miss the sharpness of Giōna's chin, the way
her cheek-bones were too prominent, and the dark
shadows under her eyes.

He held out his hand, saying as he did so with a
smile that was irresistible:

"Come along. Once you know my grandmother, you
will know that she is not so frightening as she may at
first appear."

Giōna wished she could believe him, and he thought
as they walked along the corridor that she was telling
herself that nothing could be worse than what she had
suffered at Stamford Towers.

The Duke opened a door and for a moment Giōna
could only see the golden sunlight and smell the fragrance of flowers.

Then she was able to focus her eyes on the elderly
woman with white hair.

The Duchess held out her hand.

"My grandson has been telling me about you, Giōna,"
she said, "and I hope you will enjoy staying here with
me."

Giōna curtseyed.

Then as her fingers touched the Duchess's she knew that they gave her the same feeling of safety and security that she had felt with the Duke.

"I am . . . afraid of . . . being a . . . nuisance to you, Ma'am," she replied in a nervous little voice.

"I think actually you are going to bring me a new excitement," the Duchess said. "I am already intrigued and at the same time very compassionate about what I have heard of you, and my grandson has given me very strict instructions about what we are to do in the next few weeks."

Giōna looked at the Duke enquiringly and he said:

"First of all, although it may not interest you, I have suggested that my grandmother and you choose the gowns which you should be wearing as your father's daughter."

He was quite certain as he spoke that no woman, young or old, could resist the idea of a whole new wardrobe of fashionable gowns, and he waited for the excitement to light Giōna's eyes and he was not disappointed.

"New . . . gowns?"

"Dozens of them!" the Duchess said firmly. "And as my grandson is footing the bill, we need not spare any expense!"

The light in Giōna's eyes dimmed for a moment.

"But . . . Ma'am . . . I do not . . . think I can . . ."

"You will be able to pay me back," the Duke said quietly, "when I prove as I intend to do that all the money your father left is yours and I have made sure it is refunded to you."

For a moment Giōna was speechless.

She knew that the Duke was telling her she would receive not only her father's money but the assurance that she was legitimately born, and her voice trembled and broke as she cried:

"I know . . . now you are not . . . Perseus or St.

Michael . . . but Apollo bringing . . . light and . . . healing to the world as he drives his . . . chariot across the . . . sky."

Before she could prevent them, the tears of happiness which filled her eyes ran down her cheeks.

Chapter Five

The Duke, sitting down at his desk in the Library after breakfast, found a pile of letters awaiting him.

Some of them which were official documents and invitations had already been opened by Mr. Middleton, but those that were private and personal were always placed in a separate pile.

He saw that the top two were from ladies who were endeavouring to engage his interest but for whom at the moment he had little time.

He picked up the one beneath, and, realising it was in his grandmother's hand-writing, he opened it with an eagerness that was unusual.

For two weeks now he had had no news of what was happening at the Dower House, and he had deliberately refrained from sending a groom with a note or asking his Secretary to make enquiries on his behalf.

He told himself it was most important that there should be as little connection as possible between him and Gióna until he was ready to expose her uncle.

Although he was sure he could trust his own servants, there was always the chance that some careless remark or an inquisitive underling would start the ball of gossip rolling.

He was in fact extremely anxious that Sir Jarvis

should not be suspicious that he was aware of Giōna's whereabouts.

He knew that Sir Jarvis was perturbed and bewildered by the behaviour of the Viscount.

Lucien had informed his Guardian that he had been receiving invitation after invitation to Stamford House in Grosvenor Square, and he had also had several notes from Claribel which, although he did not say so, were obviously of a passionate nature.

The Duke thought with satisfaction that, if nothing else, he and Lucien had Sir Jarvis and his disreputable daughter puzzled and perhaps more than a little apprehensive as to what had gone wrong.

Now he drew out the thick parchment paper which was engraved with the Alverstode crest, on which his grandmother had written to him in her spidery but always legible hand-writing, and read:

My dearest Grandson:

I think it is time You paid me a Visit, and I have something to show You which I am sure You will find Interesting and in fact Intriguing.

May I suggest that it might be a good Idea to bring Lucien with You? I understand He is behaving as might be Expected, which at the same time is good neither for His reputation nor for His health.

Come as soon as You can, and I shall welcome You with the deepest Delight.

I remain,
Your most affectionate
Grandmother,
Charlotte Alverstode.

The Duke smiled as he finished the letter and thought it was so typical of his grandmother that she was aware of what was happening in London and was in consequence as concerned about Lucien as he was himself.

As she had said, it was to be expected that after the shock of Claribel's perfidy he should repair his broken heart in an orgy of riotous living.

The Duke had been regaled by his friends and a number of interfering well-wishers with an almost daily account of what Lucien was doing.

There was nothing particularly reprehensible about it, except that riotous behaviour in public places, even though they were only low dance-halls and brothels, was never desirable.

He was also drinking too heavily and as usual not taking enough exercise, which resulted in his having a "Byronesque" pallor with lines of dissipation under his eyes.

It then struck the Duke that the reason his grandmother had asked him specially to bring Lucien to the Dower House was not perhaps the obvious one.

He had often heard her say in her worldly-wise manner that the "antidote for one love-affair is another," and he thought now that what she was suggesting, while being too discreet to put it on paper, was that Giōna would erase the memory of Claribel's beauty from his mind.

It occurred to the Duke that it was something he should have thought of himself.

Lucien and Giōna were the right age for each other, and what could be a better punishment for Claribel than that her despised cousin should marry the man on whom she had set her own ambitious sights?

There was a smile of satisfaction on the Duke's lips as he put down his grandmother's letter and rang the gold bell that was on his desk.

The door opened almost immediately and Mr. Middleton came into the Library.

"Send a groom to His Lordship's lodgings, Middleton," he said, "with a note asking him to accompany me to the country this afternoon. Tell His Lordship we will have a light luncheon here first, and beg him not to be late."

"I will do that, Your Grace," Mr. Middleton replied.

"Get the groom off as quickly as possible," the Duke ordered, "then we must settle down to these letters."

The letters did not take as long as he had anticipated, and the Duke had time to think further on his grandmother's idea, as he supposed, that Lucien should fall in love with Giōna.

He imagined it would not be difficult as Lucien was invariably enamoured of any outstandingly beautiful young woman.

The Duke vaguely remembered that in the past he had appeared to have a *penchant* for fair-haired charmers, but that might just have been a coincidence.

However, as a connoisseur of beauty, he was certain that he was not mistaken in thinking that once she had put on a little weight and was well-dressed, Giōna would look sensational.

He was far too diplomatic to make any suggestions to Lucien of anything more than that he thought it important they should both visit his grandmother and talk to Giōna.

"Have you learnt anything of importance about that swine Stamford?" Lucien asked aggressively.

He had arrived looking as usual a "Tulip of Fashion," but one glance at him was enough to tell the Duke that he had obviously been drinking heavily the night before and had doubtless had little sleep.

He ate practically nothing of the delicious luncheon the Chef had prepared, and the Duke made no comment when instead he drank several glasses of brandy.

Then as they were finishing luncheon Mr. Middleton came hurrying into the Dining-Room.

The servants had served the coffee and withdrawn, but nevertheless, as it was unusual for him to be disturbed at meal-times, the Duke looked up in surprise as his Secretary walked quickly across the floor.

"I thought you would want to know at once, Your Grace," Mr. Middleton said, "that our enquiries in the Dover area have been successful!"

"You mean they have discovered where the marriage of James Stamford and Elizabeth Hamilton took place?"

"Exactly, Your Grace! Here are the papers."

Mr. Middleton held out several papers to the Duke, which he took and read, thinking as he did so how thrilled Giōna would be.

She had been right, and her odious uncle had deliberately, the Duke was sure, called her a bastard just to make her unhappy.

Her parents had been married in a small village on the outskirts of Dover on 9 August 1799, as a copy of the Church Register attested.

"Good!" he exclaimed with satisfaction. "Thank you, Middleton. This is certainly one step in the right direction."

"What else have you unearthed?" Lucien asked. "Surely by now you have ferreted out something tangible about that blaggard!"

"I must ask you, My Lord, to be patient for a little while longer," Mr. Middleton replied. "I have three of the best men obtainable in Liverpool at the present moment."

"Liverpool!" the Duke exclaimed.

"My informants tell me that the scandal which Your Grace thought you remembered took place in Liverpool."

"Why there?" Lucien enquired.

"Because, My Lord, it was connected with the slave-trade, and a great number of the slave-ships were sent out from and returned to Liverpool."

The Duke sat upright.

"Are you telling me, Middleton, that Sir Jarvis's huge fortune came from slavery?"

"That is so, Your Grace, and while his father made a fortune before him, Sir Jarvis increased it a hundred-fold!"

"I might have guessed it!" the Duke said contemptuously.

"There was nothing criminal in the traffic at the time," Mr. Middleton said respectfully, "not if it was straight and above-board."

Lucien was listening intently.

"So what he did, and what Cousin Valerian thinks he remembers," he said, as if he was working it out for himself, "was something criminal."

"That is what we have to prove," Mr. Middleton replied, "but I think My Lord, in just a few more days I will be able to put in front of His Grace a statement proving that Sir Jarvis acted in both a shameful and an illegal manner."

The Duke pushed his chair back from the table and crossed his legs.

"I want the details now, Middleton!"

"No, please, Your Grace!" Mr. Middleton pleaded. "I have no wish to raise Your Grace's hopes only to be unable at the last moment to produce any evidence."

He looked pleadingly at the Duke and went on:

"We have, as Your Grace well knows, a wily and cunning man to deal with, who will use every means fair or foul to wriggle out of any trap we set for him unless it is one made of cast-iron."

"I understand," the Duke said. "Have it your own way, Middleton. But quite frankly I am eager to go ahead, and I find it very frustrating to be obliged to see Sir Jarvis on every Race-Course and sporting it in a number of decent Clubs."

"I hope when you have finished with him he will never again be able to show his face in any place which is patronised by gentlemen!" Lucien said vehemently.

He was speaking against Sir Jarvis, but the Duke was

aware that he was hating Claribel with the violence of a man who has been betrayed.

At the same time, he thought sympathetically that he was sure Lucien was still hurt and scarred by a love that in its own way had been idealistic and therefore did not die so easily.

He rose to his feet.

"Come along, Lucien," he said, "let us go to the country. At least there the air is clean and the sun is shining."

The Viscount did not seem particularly enthusiastic at the thought of encountering such pleasures. At the same time, he obediently followed his Guardian from the Dining-Room and ten minutes later they were on their way.

The Duke was driving his chestnuts and as usual they gave him so much pleasure that for a little while he forgot the unhappy young man sitting beside him.

Then he was sure that his grandmother in her wisdom had been right to send for him.

The drive to Alverstode took a little more than two hours at the rate at which the Duke travelled.

As he swung into the drive of his grandmother's Dower House, he knew that if he had not broken his own record he had certainly been only a few seconds outside it.

The mellow red-brick Queen Anne house was very lovely in the afternoon sunshine, and the Duke, appreciating its perfect symmetry, thought he might say the same about Giōna's features, especially her straight little nose.

He drew up his horses outside the front door, and as he and Lucien stepped down from the Phaeton, a groom appeared from the stables and Simpson was standing at the top of the steps to welcome them.

"I hardly dared hope that Your Grace'd be here afore tomorrow," Simpson said.

"I hoped to surprise Her Grace," the Duke replied. "Where is she?"

The Duke thought the Butler would say that she was upstairs, but instead Simpson answered:

"In the Drawing-Room, Your Grace, and Miss Giōna is with her."

That was all the Duke wished to know, and he strode across the Hall too quickly for Simpson to keep up with him and opened the door of the Drawing-Room himself.

Dramatically he stood still for a moment in the doorway and waited for the cry of welcome he expected from his grandmother.

She was sitting in the sunlight at the open window with Giōna beside her and exclaimed:

"Oh, Valerian, I am so glad to see you!"

The Duke moved forward and as he did so Giōna ran to him.

He had a quick glimpse of eyes that were shining as if the sun had been caught in them, of hair of a strange colour arranged in a fashionable manner, and of a white gown decorated with frills and flowers.

Then her hands were holding on to his and she was saying with a lilt in her voice that sounded like the song of the birds:

"You have . . . come! I have so . . . longed to see you . . . and now . . . you are here!"

She made it sound like a paean of joy and the Duke smiled as he said:

"Can this really be Giōna, or am I being introduced to a strange young woman?"

Giōna laughed, and then as if he rebuked her for being so impetuous she dropped him a respectful curtsey.

"I am deeply honoured to meet Your Grace!" she said demurely, but her eyes were twinkling.

"Let me look at you," the Duke said.

She was not in the least shy, but threw out her arms, crying:

"Yes, please look! Your grandmother and I have been so anxious to gain your approval."

She was gowned in the height of fashion, but the Duke found it difficult to take his eyes from her face.

He could see that the sharp lines of her chin and cheek-bones had already softened, while the sparkle in her eyes and the sheen in her hair told him that proper feeding and a feeling of security and happiness were working the miracle for which he had hoped.

He did not speak, and after a moment Giōna asked anxiously:

"You are not . . . disappointed?"

"How could I be?" the Duke replied. "Grandmama has waved a magic wand!"

As he spoke he found that his grandmother was being greeted by Lucien, who had entered the room behind him.

"I am delighted to see you, dear boy," she said, "and now I want you to meet my guest, whom I think you have heard about but never actually seen."

"No, I have never seen her before," Lucien replied.

He held out his hand, and as Giōna curtseyed, his smile swept away much of the signs of dissipation on his face.

The Duke somewhat belatedly kissed his grandmother's cheek, saying as he did so:

"I presume you have spent a fortune!"

"Then you presume right," she replied, "and Giōna and I intend to spend a great deal more."

"Only if . . . I can . . . afford it," Giōna said in a quiet voice before the Duke could reply.

He knew there was a question behind what she said, and in reply he put his hand under her arm and drew her towards the French windows which opened onto the terrace.

"May I leave Lucien to entertain you for a few minutes, Grandmama?" he asked. "I have something of importance that I wish to tell Giōna alone."

"There is a lot I want Lucien to tell me," the Duchess replied, and she smiled at the Viscount in a manner that was still irresistible, despite her age.

"I am so sorry for all the cruel and unnecessary suffering you have been forced to endure," she said softly.

The Duke guessed as he drew Giōna away that by the time they returned Lucien would have poured out his miseries, and as it was to somebody so sympathetic and compassionate as his grandmother, it would do him a great deal of good.

His knowledge of men told him that what Lucien found even worse than the frustration of having to wait for their revenge on Sir Jarvis was that he was unable to confide in any of his usual friends.

They would undoubtedly have plied him with questions as to why he was no longer interested in Claribel and were mystified by his behaviour, which was wilder and more outrageous than it had ever been before.

And yet there was no plausible explanation he could make to them, nothing he could say to excuse his excesses.

"Grandmama will comfort him," the Duke told himself.

He drew Giōna through the French windows and down through the rose-garden to where there was an arbour covered with honeysuckle and roses.

They reached the arbour and there were comfortable silk cushions waiting for them on the seat.

The Duke sat down and turned sideways so that he could look at Giōna, thinking as he did so that she was now not only one of the loveliest young women he had ever seen but also the most unusual.

He had been half-afraid that once she was dressed fashionably, the Greek look which he admired might vanish or at least be diminished.

Instead, she looked even more Greek, and her grey

eyes looking at him held the same adoration which he would have missed if it had not been there.

"What have you to . . . tell me?" she asked breathlessly.

"I have something to give you," the Duke replied.

As he spoke he handed her the papers that Mr. Middleton had given him just before he left London.

As she took them from him he thought her fingers were trembling, and as she read what the papers contained he saw the quiver of excitement and happiness which ran through her.

For some seconds it was, he knew, impossible for her to speak. Then at length, in a voice so low he could barely hear it, she said:

"It was true . . . I knew it . . . was!"

"It was a great help that you knew the exact month and year and that you thought it was in the vicinity of Dover."

She read what was written on the papers again and again, as if to reassure herself that what she had longed for was actually written down.

Then after a moment she raised her grey eyes and he felt as if the light in them was almost blinding.

"How . . . can you have . . . done this for . . . me?" she asked. "And how can I . . . thank you?"

"I knew it would make you happy."

"Far happier than I can possibly say. Although I knew it was untrue, the mere fact that Uncle Jarvis could jeer at my darling mother and disparage her made me feel as if I were being pelted with mud."

"And now you are flying away to the very top of Olympus," the Duke said with a smile.

"Not away from . . . you," Giōna said quickly, "because . . . without you I would . . . feel afraid."

He knew what she was thinking, and he said quietly:

"It is only a question of a little more waiting and a little more time before your uncle will be discredited and never again will he be able to menace you."

"I . . . I cannot believe that is . . . true."

"Then trust me," the Duke said. "In the meantime, as you well know, you must stay here with my grandmother and nobody must be aware of your true identity."

"Her Grace has been so wonderfully kind to me . . . and I am very happy. At the same time, I am still afraid that I may have put . . . you in a . . . dangerous position."

"You are still thinking of me?"

"Of course," she replied. "Could I think of . . . anything else when if you had not . . . rescued me I might by this time be . . . dead?"

There was a little throb as she said the last word and he knew it was still a very real fear.

"You have to forget the past," he said, "just as Lucien has to forget what happened to him. I therefore suggest that you be kind to him. He needs your help."

"Your grandmother told me that he has been behaving in a somewhat wild manner. I can understand that he has been trying to hide his suffering from other people."

"That is true," the Duke agreed. "At the same time it is not doing him any good, and, if you get the chance, I think you might try to give him a new interest."

He was aware that she looked at him enquiringly but she did not ask any more questions. Instead she said:

"Please tell me what . . . you have been . . . doing and what is the latest news from Parliament."

The Duke was surprised that she should be interested, but he told her of the Bills that were being passed through the House of Lords and the speech he intended to make about one of them.

"Is His Majesty's health really bad?" she asked when he had finished speaking.

"Very bad," the Duke replied, "and I cannot think that he will live much longer."

"Then the Regent will be King," Giōna said, "and I think that recently, because I have had to wait as he has had to do, I began to understand that nothing is more difficult than what Papa called 'possessing one's soul in patience'!"

The Duke laughed.

"Is that what you are doing?"

"I do not know about my soul," Giōna replied, "but my mind is very, very impatient, and it makes my body nervous and restless."

"Nevertheless," he smiled, "it is now very elegantly adorned, and you look very different from the little grey shadow I found sitting on a tree-trunk."

"Always in my dreams," Giōna answered, "I see you walking towards me. I know now, even if I did not . . . realise it at the time, that you were . . . enveloped in the . . . light of Apollo."

"It sounds very poetical," the Duke said lightly.

"It is, and that is why . . ."

Giōna stopped.

The Duke looked at her enquiringly. Then he asked:

"Have you been writing a poem about what happened?"

There was a faint flush on her cheeks as she answered:

"I did not mean to tell you . . . but it is a poem to . . . you. I merely tried to . . . express what I feel about . . . you in verse because it is easier than in prose."

"I am honoured," the Duke said. "When may I see it?"

"Never!"

He looked surprised and she explained:

"It is so inadequate. There are no words even in poetry to describe you, and when I have written a page I tear it up . . . ashamed that I am . . . unable to convey adequately what I am . . . feeling in . . . words."

"Perhaps it is the language that is at fault," the Duke suggested. "Try writing in Greek."

She gave a little cry and clasped her hands together.

"What a wonderful idea! It is something I shall do, then I think I will not be so embarrassed to show it to you."

"I shall be waiting to read it," the Duke said.

As he spoke he wondered if there was any other woman of his acquaintance now or in the past who could have written a poem about him in Greek.

Then he told himself that he must encourage Giōna to concentrate not on him but on Lucien.

As they walked in the garden he said:

"Now do as I tell you. Try to help Lucien. It may eventually do him good to have loved and lost, but for the moment he is finding it a very painful experience."

* * *

It was a great surprise to the Duke that his grandmother was well enough to dine downstairs with them, and later that evening he watched Giōna walk onto the terrace and a second later Lucien joined her.

They were leaning on the stone balustrade and had started to talk quietly to each other. The Duke could not hear what they said, but there was no doubt that Lucien was speaking eagerly in a voice that was very different from the sullen drawl that was all his Guardian had heard for the last fortnight.

"They make a very charming couple," the Duchess said complacently.

"They are certainly both very good-looking," the Duke replied.

"Giōna has all the stability and intelligence that a young man like Lucien needs," the Duchess went on. "She is a very sweet creature, the servants all adore her, and every dog and horse in the place will come if she calls them."

"She is certainly exceptional," the Duke agreed.

"It has made me very happy to have her here. In fact I feel better than I have felt for years."

"I have always said there is nothing wrong with you, Grandmama, except boredom."

"Well, nobody can be bored with Giōna," the Duch-

ess said, "and even if she had not such an intriguing
story which makes her like a heroine in a novelette, I
should still find her adorable."

The Duke knew this was very high praise from his
grandmother, who seldom liked young women, and he
thought that with such attributes it would be very
surprising if Lucien was not soon "off with the old love
and on with the new."

He looked and found that they had left the terrace
while he had talked to his grandmother and were now
out of sight.

He told himself that was just what he had been
hoping for, and then as he saw that the sun was sinking
low in a blaze of glory he remembered that was how it
had been when he had first seen Giōna, seated on the
fallen trunk of a tree.

He had known then when he spoke to her that she
was very different from what she appeared and even in
her ugly grey gown she had been beautiful.

He glanced through the window. Soon the stars
would be coming out and the last glow from the sun
would have disappeared behind the trees.

Suddenly he remembered how as he had looked at
Giōna the moonlight had revealed the look of adoration
in her eyes.

He wondered what she and Lucien were saying to
each other and if she was looking at him in the same
way.

For some reason he could not understand, he suddenly
felt extremely irritated.

It made him rise to his feet to walk to the table
where Simpson had left a decanter of brandy and
several glasses.

Without speaking the Duke poured himself out a
glass of brandy, and with the glass in his hand he turned
and walked across the room to stand looking out into
the garden.

He supposed that by this time Giōna and Lucien would be seated in the arbour where there was the fragrance of honeysuckle and roses.

In the twilight it would be very romantic, and he wondered what Lucien was doing.

Was he frightening her by being over-impetuous? Or was he expressing his admiration too fervently?

"Dammit all!" the Duke muttered beneath his breath. "He might even try to kiss her!"

At the thought, there was a feeling rising inside him which was different from anything he had ever felt before.

He could not explain it to himself, nor did he wish to. He only knew that it was a mistake for Giōna to be alone in the garden with a man she had only just met, besides being extremely unconventional.

The Duke put down his glass of brandy untouched.

"I think, Grandmama, I will take a stroll outside," he said. "I feel it is very airless in here."

"Why, of course, dearest! I agree with you. It has been very hot today."

Without waiting for her reply, he was already walking out onto the terrace and down the steps which led to the lawn, and his footsteps seemed to ring out on the stones.

His grandmother watched him, a slightly puzzled expression in her shrewd old eyes. She had summed up a great number of men one way or another in the passing years.

Then, as if a new idea had come to her, there was a faint smile on her lips and she sat back a little more comfortably in her chair to await the return of her guests.

* * *

The Duke walked casually, as he told himself, towards the arbour but when he reached it he found it was empty.

He was surprised.

"Where the devil have they gone?" he wondered.

Giōna and Lucien had in fact walked on from the rose-garden into the herb-garden and from there towards the Maze.

When they reached it Lucien said:

"I hated that Maze when I was a small boy because it frightened me. Now I think I hate it because it is like my life: a lot of paths which end abruptly and make me realise I have wasted my time exploring them."

He spoke bitterly and Giōna said:

"If one always got exactly what one wanted at the first attempt, think how dull it would be."

"Dull?"

"Of course, and one would just give up trying."

She felt that the Viscount did not understand, and she explained:

"Suppose you always knew what horse was going to win the race? What would be the point of watching it? If you shot down every bird you aimed at, it would hardly be worthwhile going out shooting. It is the same with other things in life. I think failures only make one keener to succeed."

"I suppose I understand what you are saying," Lucien said, "but it is a very different thing when one is disillusioned with—people."

"The point is that we should not blame them but ourselves."

The Viscount looked at her in astonishment.

"Do you believe that?"

"Of course! I believe that our instinct is one of the most precious things we possess. If we are deceived by a person's character, that is our stupidity—for we should never expect from people more than they are capable of giving."

She paused.

"Go on," the Viscount prompted. "I am trying to follow you."

"Our failures are rather like flowers which fade too quickly, so we throw them away. But there are thousands of others waiting for us to pick them. It is, if you think about it, very exciting when one has such a variety of choice."

The Viscount stared at her. Then he laughed.

"You are extraordinary, and not in the least like any other girl I have ever met."

Giōna smiled.

"If that is true, it must be the result of my foreign travels. The world makes one realise what exciting people there are in a dozen different nations, and the only sadness is that there is not enough time in one's life to get to know them all."

"I believe Cousin Valerian did tell me you had lived abroad."

"I have travelled a great deal," Giōna said, "and it is something you should do."

She saw that the idea had not occurred to Lucien, and she went on:

"I cannot tell you how wonderful India is and how different from any other place in the world. It is not only the Indians themselves, who are beautiful with charming good manners, but there are so many creeds and castes that every day one learns something from them, as from the country itself."

She looked up at the sunset.

"To me, India is crimson and gold. It is shining and mysterious, and it is a mystery that is part of one's heart and soul and always of one's mind."

She spoke almost as if she was inspired.

Then as he looked at her the Viscount asked:

"What is stopping me from seeing for myself and perhaps feeling as you do about it?"

"If you can afford it—visit India," Giōna said. "Money is the only stumbling-block for most people."

The Viscount gave a sudden cry.

"You have solved it!" he said. "You have answered the

question that has been haunting me these past two weeks."

"What question?" Giōna asked.

"What I should do with myself," he replied, "and, if I am honest, how I can—forget."

He spoke the last word in a low voice, and Giōna said quickly:

"I thought you would be feeling like that. That is why you should go away."

"Of course I should," the Viscount agreed, "but I could not think where to go, and I do not want to be alone in any other part of England."

"No, of course not!" Giōna said. "It would only make you miserable and you will keep regretting the past, which is something you must not do."

She looked towards the sunset as she said:

"A new future is waiting there for you, strange, exciting, different from anything you have ever seen or known before. But if you do not find India as wonderful as I anticipate you will, then there are many other countries which will give you new ideas and I think too new ambitions."

The Viscount drew in his breath. Then he said:

"Thank you. You have shown me the centre of the Maze, and now I know I can find my way!"

Giōna turned to smile at him, and he took her hand in his and raised it to his lips.

"Thank you," he said again as he kissed it.

* * *

As he came round the corner of a yew-hedge the Duke saw Giōna and Lucien standing at the entrance to the Maze and the graceful stance of the Viscount as he kissed Giōna's hand.

It struck him that it would be impossible for two people to look more elegant or more romantic, but their appearance gave him no pleasure.

Instead, an emotion something like anger seemed to

burn through him, making him feel as if he saw them both coloured as crimson as the sunset.

Then, because he was intelligent he knew, undeniably, incredibly, and utterly unexpectedly, that what he was feeling was jealousy!

Chapter Six

The Duke spent a restless night trying to convince himself that what he had felt when he saw Lucien kissing Giōna's hand was not jealousy. He told himself he must have drunk too much at dinner, or else was feeling on edge at having so little news of Sir Jarvis.

Whatever it was, the idea was ridiculous! How could he at his age be concerned with a girl of eighteen?

He had already assured himself not once but a dozen times that his concern for Giōna was entirely impersonal.

His real object was to bring Sir Jarvis to justice both for his treatment of what was little more than a child and for the manner in which both he and his daughter had been prepared to deceive Lucien.

But try as he would, it was impossible for him not to find himself a dozen times a day thinking of Giōna, of her strange Grecian beauty and the expression in her eyes when she looked at him.

He tried to tell himself as he drove back to Alverstode House that whatever his feelings over Lucien had been, they were unnecessary.

Then as they moved along the narrow lanes which lay between the Dower House and Alverstode itself, Lucien remarked:

"I have decided to go to India!"

"To India?" the Duke exclaimed in surprise. "What makes you think of going there?"

"Giōna has convinced me that it would be a good idea, and I want to get away."

There was a pause of some seconds before the Duke asked:

"Is she thinking of accompanying you?"

"No, of course not! Why should you think she would do that? Besides, I want to go alone."

"Yes, of course," the Duke agreed, "and on consideration I think it would be a good idea for you to travel."

Obviously gratified at his agreement, Lucien talked eagerly of the places he would like to visit, until they reached Alverstode House.

As the Duke was anxious that nobody should guess that Giōna was staying with his grandmother, he had made it quite clear when they left London where he and Lucien would be.

He had then remarked casually to his servants after he arrived that he was dining at the Dower House.

Because news of interest on the Estate travelled as if on the wind, he was quite certain that by this time his servants and quite a number of other people would be aware that his grandmother had a visitor.

He hoped that because there were a great number of things that required his attention at his home, nobody would connect him in any possible way with Giōna.

Yet, when he was alone he found himself thinking how lovely she looked in her new gown and it was difficult for him not to appreciate the warmth and sincerity in his grandmother's voice when she spoke of her.

One thing had come out of the evening which was unexpected: Giōna was sending Lucien away and it would therefore be difficult for anybody, even somebody as skilful as the Duchess, to encourage her to be interested in him.

"I suppose it is too soon for him to think any girl

attractive after Claribel," the Duke told himself ruefully.

Then once again there was that question in his mind as to why he had felt so strange when he saw Lucien kissing Giōna's hand.

Hibbert called him at his usual early hour and he went riding, knowing there was no question of Lucien rising early enough to join him.

He resisted an impulse to ride in the direction of the Dower House and instead galloped over the Park in the opposite direction.

Breakfast was waiting for him when he returned a little later than usual, and he was just finishing what had been a satisfying meal when the Butler announced:

"Mr. Middleton has arrived from London to see Your Grace."

"Mr. Middleton!" the Duke exclaimed in surprise.

Then before he could say any more Mr. Middleton walked into the Dining-Room.

"Good Heavens!" the Duke ejaculated. "What brings you here so early in the morning? Has the house burnt down, or have I been robbed of everything I possess?"

"Neither, Your Grace," Mr. Middleton replied.

He waited for the Butler to close the door and they were left alone in the Dining-Room before he said:

"I received news last night that I thought should be in your hands immediately."

"About Sir Jarvis?"

Mr. Middleton nodded.

"Sit down and tell me about it," the Duke invited. "Will you have a cup of coffee?"

"Thank you, that can wait," Mr. Middleton replied, "but this is urgent."

"I am sure it is. You must have left London before dawn!"

Mr. Middleton sat down at the table and drew some papers out of a brief-case.

"You were quite right, Your Grace," he said, "in

suspecting there had been some scandal, and it is in fact very much worse than we thought."

There was a look of satisfaction on the Duke's face as he settled himself in his chair to listen.

"We already knew," Mr. Middleton went on, "that Sir Jarvis's father had made a considerable amount of money out of the slave-trade, and Sir Jarvis was in it in a very big way."

"His ships, I imagine, were based at Liverpool?" the Duke interposed.

"The majority of them," Mr. Middleton agreed, "and I hardly need add that he was one of the slave-traders with a reputation for being more ruthless and more avaricious than the others."

"That is what I might have surmised," the Duke remarked.

"However, in 1800 he overstepped himself," Mr. Middleton continued. "A cargo of slaves being carried in one of Sir Jarvis's ships from Africa was, on arrival in the Port of Savannah, barred from entering the harbour because a large number of the Negroes aboard had contracted Yellow Fever."

The Duke was aware that this would have involved the strictest quarantine since Yellow Fever was notoriously infectious.

"As it happened," Mr. Middleton went on, "Sir Jarvis was actually in Savannah at the time, waiting to receive a high price for the slaves that were to be disembarked and placed in the stockade where prospective buyers could inspect them."

The Duke nodded, knowing the procedure regarding slaves which he had read in the reports put before Parliament.

"Apparently," Mr. Middleton continued, "Sir Jarvis was furious when the ship was forced to anchor outside the port, and no amount of persuasion or bribery on his part could change the authorities' ban until the ship had received medical clearance."

Mr. Middleton paused for breath, and the Duke asked:

"Then what happened?"

"Apparently, from the reports my investigators have received, Sir Jarvis suddenly changed his whole attitude and informed everybody that the precautions were very wise and the only people he was sorry for were the Captain and crew aboard the ship."

The Duke raised his eye-brows but he did not interrupt, and Mr. Middleton went on:

"In fact, he was so sorry for them that he sent several barrels of rum aboard so that they could at least enjoy themselves while they were waiting."

Mr. Middleton's voice lowered as he remarked:

"The rum must have been very potent, for that night the ship, according to my reports, was set on fire, and nobody was awake to give the alarm."

"What you are saying," the Duke said slowly, "is that the rum was drugged!"

"That is a supposition that has not been easy to prove," Mr. Middleton said. "The ship burnt quickly and there were few survivors."

"Why was that?"

"Because in Sir Jarvis's ships all the Negroes were in chains below-decks. This was not the usual practice of the trade, except in ships where there had been riots or where the wretched creatures had tried frantically to throw themselves overboard."

"So there was no chance of their getting away?"

"None survived," Mr. Middleton said, "except two of the crew, who were badly burnt."

"It is the most monstrous thing I have ever heard!" the Duke cried.

"Now we come to the main point of our investigations, Your Grace," Mr. Middleton said. "The Shipping-Company put in a large claim to the Insurance-Writers and it was they who thought the whole thing was suspicious and raised the question of arson."

The Duke made a sound but Mr. Middleton continued:

"I have been in touch with them, and they considered they had a very good case against the Shipping-Company of which Sir Jarvis was not only the Chairman but the main Share-Holder."

"Then why did they not prosecute him?" the Duke enquired.

"They were about to do so," Mr. Middleton replied, "when they found that that particular ship was solely owned by another Director of the Company."

"Who was that?"

"Sir Jarvis's brother, James Stamford!"

The Duke started.

Now he was beginning to understand the secret which had kept Giōna's father abroad for so long.

"A warrant was actually made out for the arrest of James Stamford," Mr. Middleton was saying, "but it was found that he had gone abroad the previous year, and although the warrant is still in existence it has not been executed because he never returned to this country."

"So that is how Sir Jarvis got himself out of trouble!" the Duke exclaimed harshly.

"The detectives I hired for this investigation," Mr. Middleton said, "found a man in Liverpool who retired many years ago from the firm, and they managed to persuade him to make a statement admitting that he had tampered with the documents regarding the ownership of the vessel."

"It was obviously not very difficult," the Duke observed, "to alter the name of 'Jarvis' into 'James.'"

"That is exactly what the clerk said when he was questioned," Mr. Middleton said with a smile.

"It was clever! Very clever!" the Duke murmured.

"There was quite a lot about it in the newspapers at the time," Mr. Middleton continued. "Mr. William Wilberforce asked questions in Parliament, and the

Abolition of Slavery Society spoke out violently against any ship-owner chaining slaves with the result that even if the ship was in great danger there was no possibility of their freeing themselves. However, without a scape-goat the whole controversy died down."

The Duke was seeing it all so clearly, realising how extraordinarily astute Sir Jarvis had been.

His brother James had already decided to live abroad for a time until the gossip and scandal over his marriage should subside.

That Sir Jarvis was prepared to make him a very rich man if he would save him and the family name from disgrace by continuing his exile indefinitely would not have seemed such a hardship at the beginning of his marriage, when he was wildly in love and ask-ing only to be with the woman who had captured his heart.

He could understand what Giōna had meant when she said that later her father was sometimes restless and homesick for the country of his birth and for the sports and pastimes he had always enjoyed.

What was unforgivable was that, having saved his brother from social disgrace if nothing else, Sir Jarvis had then deliberately robbed and ill-treated Giōna be-cause he was afraid that in some way she might reveal his guilty secret.

Now there was no question that he must be brought to punishment, and that was something about which the Duke was determined.

"I suppose there would be no difficulty in proving what you have just told me?" the Duke asked.

"None at all, Your Grace," Mr. Middleton replied. "It was because I am so anxious that every detail could be substantiated and that I could produce witnesses who were not only reliable but who would be accredited in Court, that this investigation has taken longer than Your Grace hoped."

"I am now extremely grateful to you, Middleton,"

the Duke said, and there was no mistaking the satisfaction in his voice.

Mr. Middleton rose from the table.

"I will put these papers on Your Grace's desk," he said, "so that you can peruse them at your leisure. There is only one thing which I must admit is slightly unfortunate."

The Duke looked at his Secretary sharply.

"And what is that?" he enquired.

"It is that I am afraid," Mr. Middleton said hesitatingly, "that Sir Jarvis by now will be aware that we are making enquiries."

"How do you know?"

"The investigators were instructed to work with the greatest possible secrecy," Mr. Middleton replied, "but the behaviour of one Senior Clerk in the firm of which Sir Jarvis is still Chairman, and the fact that he disappeared the day after people had been there, makes them suspect that he had come South to notify Sir Jarvis of what was taking place."

"That is unfortunate," the Duke said, "and I presume he may now know or at least guess that I am behind the enquiries you have been making."

"I cannot completely rule out the possibility, Your Grace."

The Duke was silent.

He was thinking of Giōna and as he did so his instinct, which had always warned him of danger during the war, told him now that if Sir Jarvis was aware that it was he who was behind the enquiries, then he would also suspect who was responsible for Giōna's disappearance.

The feeling of danger was so strong, so insistent, that he told himself it was imperative that he should see Giōna immediately to warn her not only of what had occurred but that it might even be necessary to move her somewhere else.

He rose to his feet, saying as he did so:

"Thank you, Middleton! Thank you very much! Now have some breakfast after your journey, and I will see you later in the morning."

"I thank Your Grace."

The Duke walked from the Dining-Room, and when he reached the Hall he was wondering whether to ride or to drive to the Dower House.

Then the Butler came towards him to say:

"The horses that Your Grace ordered to be brought round for Your Grace's appraisal are outside."

The Duke remembered then, which he had forgotten, that he had told his grooms when he finished riding that he wished to see a pair of bays that he had bought at Tattersall's the previous week.

"I will drive them with a High-Perch Phaeton," he had said, "and see how they work out."

Now it struck him that if he drove them to the Dower House he would be "killing two birds with one stone" and also assuaging his sense of anxiety.

Then he laughed at his fears and was sure that his feelings of danger and emergency were quite unnecessary. It was surely impossible for Sir Jarvis to guess where Giōna was hidden.

Nevertheless, there was no point in taking risks.

"I am going to the Dower House," he said to his Butler.

As he walked towards the front door Hibbert came down the stairs with a clean pair of gloves to replace those he had worn during his early-morning ride.

He had no idea why, but his instinct told him to take Hibbert with him, and without troubling to make any explanation he said:

"Come with me, Hibbert. I want you!" and walked down the steps towards the Phaeton.

Fortunately it was not Ben who was in charge of it, who would have been offended if he had been replaced by the Duke's valet, but one of the younger grooms.

The Duke swung himself into the driving-seat and

picked up the reins. Hibbert would have climbed up onto the small seat behind had not the Duke ordered him sharply to sit beside him.

The bays, which had been sold as being well-trained though spirited, set off at a sharp pace.

The Duke quickly had them under control and they moved out of the courtyard, and some way along the oak-lined drive they turned along a grass track which was the quickest route to the Dower House.

Hibbert did not speak, but the Duke knew he was alert with curiosity and had a feeling in his bones that "something was up."

But the Duke still made no explanation, saying only:

"I have the idea I may need you, Hibbert, so be ready and on your guard."

"Against what or whom, Your Grace?"

"To be honest, I have no idea," the Duke replied. "But we may be in trouble."

"I hope that's true, Your Grace," Hibbert said with a grin. "A man gets soft in peacetime."

The Duke smiled.

It was what he thought himself, but he did not trouble to answer, concerning himself with his horses.

* * *

Giōna had not slept well because she had sensed when the Duke had said good-night that something had annoyed him.

She had no idea what it would be, but there was a harsh note in his voice, his eyes looked like steel, and she thought he had retreated into a shell which made him seem impersonal and out of reach.

"What has...upset him? What could...I have... done?" she asked herself.

Although she went diligently over in her mind everything that had been said during the evening, she found no clue to the sudden change in his attitude between dinner and the time when they had said good-night.

If Lucien had not been there, she thought, she would have been brave enough to ask him if anything was wrong.

But there had really been no opportunity, and after the Duke had joined them in the garden they had immediately walked back to the house, where he had made his farewells to his grandmother.

"Shall we see you tomorrow?" the Duchess had asked.

"I have no idea," the Duke replied in a cold voice which made Gióna look at him in surprise.

"Well, Gióna and I will be waiting eagerly for your return whenever it may be," the Duchess replied. "I hoped you would have luncheon with us."

"I will think about it."

The Duke kissed his grandmother's cheek in a perfunctory fashion and walked towards the door.

He had not spoken to Gióna, but she followed him into the Hall and looked at him pleadingly as he took his tall hat from one of the servants and threw his evening-cape over his arm.

She could not help remembering how he had loaned it to her to enter the Village Inn pretending to be his sister, and she thought that if he were not in such a strange mood she would have been able to make him laugh about it.

However, he was moving to the front door while she said wistfully:

"Good-night . . . Your Grace."

He did not look at her nor turn his head. He merely replied: "Good-night!" as if he were speaking from the icy reaches of the North Pole.

"Good-night, and thank you!" Lucien said.

She wondered if he would have said more, but as if he realised he was keeping his Guardian waiting he hurried after him to jump into the closed carriage.

They drove away, and Gióna, watching until the carriage was out of sight, felt as if it carried her heart with it.

It was not until several hours later in the darkness of her bedroom that she admitted to herself that she loved the Duke.

"I love him! I love him!" she whispered into her pillow, and she knew it was like looking at the moon, or because to her the Duke was Apollo—the sun.

"He saved me . . . he brought me . . . hope and gave me a new life. How could I ask for . . . anything more?" she whispered to herself.

But she knew that in fact she wanted a great deal more from him. She wanted him as a man, she wanted him to approve of her, to admire her, and most of all to love her!

She asked herself how she could be so absurd or indeed so presumptuous, and yet the answer was very obvious.

Nobody could control love, and she was aware that it was only because she was so ignorant about it that she had not known the moment she saw him that he had taken her heart from her and it was no longer her own.

"I love . . . him! I love . . . him!"

There seemed to be nothing else to say, and she tossed and turned until the stars outside faded and the first golden fingers of the dawn crept up the sky.

It was only then that she fell asleep, with the word "love" still on her lips.

* * *

Giōna awoke early and was dressed long before it was possible for her to go to the Duchess's room.

Because the Duchess had been a beauty she could not bear anybody to see her until she had powdered and rouged her face and her hair had been arranged by her lady's-maid.

Only then, with the windows open, flowers scenting her room, and looking elegant against the lace-trimmed pillows, was the Duchess prepared to see any members of her household who wished to consult her, and of course Giōna.

"It is a lovely day!" the Dowager said when Giōna reached her bedside. "I hope that my grandson when he visits us may take you driving."

"I would love that!" Giōna exclaimed. "But perhaps he has . . . more important things to do."

"I doubt it," the Duchess said firmly, "but I wish now I had suggested it to him yesterday afternoon. You have been cooped up here long enough, and it would be quite safe for you to drive round parts of the Estate where you are not likely to be seen."

Giōna gave a little sigh.

"There are so many things I want to talk about to His Grace."

There was something so wistful in the way she spoke that the Duchess said quickly:

"I am sure he will realise that and will join us for luncheon. Tell Agnes I want to get up so that I shall be ready when he comes."

The Duchess noticed the eager way in which Giōna ran across the bedroom to find her lady's-maid, and she thought there was no doubt that the child was in love with her grandson.

It was something she had hoped would not happen because she was well aware of the Duke's reputation for loving and leaving the women who pursued him.

But last night she had changed her mind.

The Duchess had had too many love-affairs of her own not to recognise the signs when a man was jealous.

She was quite certain that the reason why the Duke had walked so purposefully into the garden and had come back with a frown between his eyes, behaving in a manner which showed that he was keeping himself strictly under control, was that his feelings towards Giōna were not only those of compassion.

The Duchess thought that any other girl of Giōna's age would be too young for an experienced, sophisticat-

ed man of twenty-nine, but she had not been with her
these past weeks without learning how intelligent she
was.

What was more, travelling all over the world had
given her a very different outlook from that of the girls
who had seen nothing but their School-Rooms before
they were pitch-forked into Society.

'Giōna does not think about herself,' the Duchess
thought, 'but about nations, peoples, politics, and reli-
gion, and those are the subjects which will keep a man
interested eventually rather than a pretty face.'

At the same time, the Duchess was apprehensive.

Nobody knew better than she did how unpredictable
her grandson could be, and who indeed could know for
certain whether what he was feeling was love or merely
boredom?

He had made Giōna his responsibility, but her apparent interest in a younger and very handsome man
might make him decide abruptly that she no longer
interested him or had any claim on him.

Then the Duchess told herself that she was sure that
was not true.

"I shall just have to wait and see," she said with a
little sigh as her lady's-maid came hurrying into the
bedroom to help her rise and dress.

Knowing it would be some time before the Duchess
appeared, Giōna walked downstairs wondering what
she should do with herself.

She knew that what she really wanted, because she
was so eager to see the Duke again, was to watch for
the appearance of his horses in the drive.

"Please, God, let him come soon!" she prayed.

It was perhaps a very trivial thing to pray for, and yet
she knew it came from her heart with an intensity she
could not control.

"Come . . . soon! Come . . . soon!"

She felt as if every step she took on the stairs
repeated the words, and that they flew towards him on

wings and he would be aware how much she needed him.

Then just before she reached the bottom of the stairs she heard the sound of wheels and thought with a leap of her heart that her prayer was already answered and the Duke was there.

Then she saw old Simpson move very slowly on his rheumaticky feet towards the open door, and a man's voice said:

"Tell Miss Stamford Oi be wantin' to speak wi' 'er."

"Miss Stamford!" Simpson exclaimed in surprise. "There's no-one here of that name."

"Aye, there be," the man said. "Oi means the young lady as be a-stayin' 'ere."

"Miss Andreas? Is that whom you're referring to?" Simpson enquired.

"Tha's right. Tell 'er t' come to the door."

When Giōna had heard the man ask for her she had stood still and now was standing on the bottom step of the stairs and holding on to the bannister.

She thought with a sudden contraction of her heart that something was wrong.

Then it flashed into her mind that only one person would call her by her rightful name, and that was her uncle.

Wildly she thought she must hide, but as she was about to turn and run back up the stairs, Simpson looked in her direction, aware that she was there, and the man to whom he was talking saw her too.

"Tha' be 'er!" he said in a voice that seemed to ring out.

Before Giōna could move, before she could turn round and run up the stairs, he had stepped into the Hall and picked her up in his arms.

She gave a scream of terror, but before she could protest or realise what was happening, he ran down the steps with her and, lifting her up, bundled her onto the seat of a High-Perch Phaeton.

As she gave another scream of sheer fright and terror, she realised who was driving the horses and felt her voice die against her lips.

"Tie her in, Jake!" Sir Jarvis said harshly, and the man fastened a thick leather strap round her waist, which held her imprisoned to the back of the seat.

Then he stepped back and swung himself up into the seat behind as Sir Jarvis whipped up his horses and they were off.

"What . . . are you . . . doing? Where are you . . . taking me?" Giōna tried to gasp, but her voice was incoherent.

Her uncle turned his eyes from the horses he was driving to look at her, and she thought the expression on his face was the most terrifying and evil thing she had ever seen.

"I am taking you back where you belong," he said, "and I will make sure that you not only never escape again but regret having made any attempt to do so!"

"Y-you have . . . no right to do this . . . to me . . ." Giōna tried to say.

"I have every right," Sir Jarvis replied grimly. "I am your Guardian, and you will certainly cease to talk of 'rights' by the time I have finished with you!"

There was something so ominous in the way he spoke that Giōna felt almost as if he drained away her life from her and already she was dying as she had been when the Duke had rescued her.

She wondered how her uncle could have discovered where she was, what the Duke would do when he found that she had gone, and if she would ever see him again.

She knew Sir Jarvis did not speak lightly when he told her he would make sure she would be unable to escape another time, and she knew without him putting it into words what treatment would be awaiting her at Stamford Towers.

As if he was aware of what she was thinking, he said:

"Just as you are strapped into this Phaeton beside

me, so in future I will see that you are chained to the
wall of your room. You will be treated like a prisoner,
Giōna, and you will receive the same punishment as
any felon or criminal, for that is what you are."

Giōna shut her eyes.

The way her uncle spoke made her feel that she was
already enduring the whip-lashes she would undoubtedly
receive later, and she only hoped that if he intended to
kill her, as she was sure he did, he would do so quickly.

Then to her surprise she realised that Sir Jarvis was
slowing his horses.

She opened her eyes and saw that they were in a
narrow lane where the branches of the trees met overhead.

It was like a tunnel except that the sunshine was
percolating through the leaves, making a pattern of gold
which she would have thought beautiful if she had not
been so terrified.

"Is this the right place, Jake?" Sir Jarvis asked the
man who was sitting behind him.

As he spoke, another man appeared from the bushes
beside the road, and as she looked at him Giōna saw
that he was exceptionally burly and thick-set.

There was something about him which made her
think of a prize-fighter, and she was sure that was what
he was. A moment later he was joined by the man who
had been sitting behind her uncle.

Giōna stared at them in terror and knew that her first
supposition was right.

They were pugilists, and because neither of them was
wearing a coat she could see their muscles bulging
beneath the cotton shirts which they wore with handkerchiefs round their necks.

"Give me a hand with the horses," Sir Jarvis said
sharply.

The man called Jake did as he was told and pulled
the horses across so that the Phaeton now blocked the
lane completely.

When this had been done to Sir Jarvis's satisfaction, the horses put down their heads and started to crop the grass, which to Giōna's surprise he allowed them to do.

Then he thrust his left hand, which was nearest to her, into the pocket of the riding-coat he wore.

She had been too frightened to look at him until now, and she realised that it was a tiered caped coat in which she had seen him before, but she wondered why he needed it as it was a warm day.

As his hand went into the pocket he appeared to be testing something, and with a frightened stab of her heart she was sure it was a pistol.

Then he took the reins in his left hand and drew from the other pocket of his coat a second pistol, which he looked at to see that it was cocked before he put it back in his pocket.

"What . . . are you doing? What are you . . . waiting for?" Giōna asked.

She thought her uncle would not answer her question, but he replied:

"I thought you would like, my dear niece, to see me destroy the man who has taken it upon himself, doubtless at your instigation, to menace my security."

Giōna gave a little gasp and he went on:

"This, of course, is something I cannot allow, and so as you have interfered and aroused his curiosity, you will watch him die!"

"W-what are you . . . talking about? What are you . . . saying?" Giōna asked frantically.

"You know what I am saying," Sir Jarvis said. "It will of course be very unfortunate that the most noble Duke—such a handsome man!—should have been set upon by Highwaymen—such an unscrupulous lot—and left for dead on his own land."

The way he spoke made Giōna give a scream of sheer terror.

"How can you . . . consider such a . . . thing? . . . How

can you want to . . . kill anybody . . . least of all the Duke?"

"If he dies it will upset you, and that is why, you tiresome little bastard, I have brought you here to witness his death!"

"How can you . . . do such a . . . thing? And it was not . . . true what you . . . told me! Papa and Mama *were* married! I have seen the . . . record of it!"

Giōna almost shouted the words at him, and once again Sir Jarvis looked at her with an expression of such loathing that she shrank away from him as far as the strap round her waist would allow her to do.

"So the inquisitive Duke has found that out? That is another reason for me to exterminate him, just as I intend later to exterminate you!"

"You are mad!" Giōna gasped. "But if I must die . . . please do not . . . kill him! He was . . . only being kind . . . and helpful."

"Very kind and very helpful!" Sir Jarvis mocked. "And anxious, I understand, to bring me to justice, which is something I have no intention of allowing."

"Talk to him . . . beg him to . . . spare you," Giōna pleaded, "but . . . please do not kill him."

"Because you are obviously besotted with the man," Sir Jarvis said, "I know now I was right in thinking that it would perturb you to watch his execution. And what could be more appropriate than that you should be wearing the finery that he has obviously paid for while you do so."

His eyes travelled over her gown, then came back to her face as he said:

"You obviously wish to look your best for the Duke, but let me tell you something: Before he appears, if you scream or make any attempt to warn him, I will smash this pistol into your face so that in the future no man will look at you except in horror!"

He saw the terror in Giōna's eyes and added:

"A broken nose and no teeth are not attractive! No, Giōna, you will be silent."

"Please ... please ..." Giōna began, wanting desperately to plead not for herself but for the Duke.

Then Jake, looking up the road ahead of him, exclaimed: "Oi finks he be a-comin', Guv'!"

"Then do exactly as I told you," Sir Jarvis ordered.

Giōna saw the other man draw a pistol from his pocket.

Giōna held her breath.

She could hear as distinctly as Jake had the sounds of horses' hoofs in the distance, until round the corner a little way ahead of them she saw first a pair of perfectly matched horses and a second later the man who was driving them.

There was no mistaking the angle at which the Duke wore his riding-hat or the breadth of his shoulders in his tight-fitting, grey whip-cord jacket.

He must have seen them as soon as they saw him, for he began to draw in his horses. Then as they drew nearer, Giōna saw that Hibbert was sitting beside him and wondered frantically what she should do.

She knew that her uncle had not spoken idly when he had said he would smash her face with his pistol. But she told herself that that was immaterial if she could save the Duke's life.

She was sure there was not a remote possibility that while driving on his own Estate he would be carrying a pistol with him.

Having broken her nose and teeth as her uncle had threatened, he would still shoot and kill an unarmed man.

"What ... shall I do? What shall I ... do?" Giōna asked herself frantically, and could only watch with terrified eyes as the Duke came nearer and nearer.

As he finally brought his horses to a standstill he saw Sir Jarvis waiting for him and also Giōna.

"Good-morning, Your Grace!" Sir Jarvis said mockingly.

"I imagine you are waiting to speak to me," the Duke replied. "Do you intend that we shall shout at each other, or shall we alight and talk in a more civilised manner?"

"As you have somebody to hold your reins," Sir Jarvis replied, "and I do not wish to trust my niece with my cattle, I suggest you come to me."

As her uncle spoke, Giōna realised that Jake must have hidden himself, and though she wanted to cry out that the Duke must not alight, she could not for the moment see what she would gain by doing so.

The Duke handed Hibbert the reins, and as he alighted, the second prize-fighter came from behind the bushes with his pistol in his hand, pointing it at the valet.

Then, so swiftly that it made Giōna catch her breath, Jake rushed at the Duke and attempted to strike at him.

The Duke was taken by surprise, yet he avoided the blow which undoubtedly would have knocked him down, and it only brushed the sleeve of his coat while his top-hat fell from his head.

Then the two men were fighting in a manner which showed Giōna that they were both extremely proficient and experienced pugilists.

For a moment she was terrified that another blow from Jake would send the Duke spread-eagled on the ground.

She had been aware of his strength when he had carried her as if she were nothing but a doll down the steps and lifted her into the Phaeton.

She could see the huge muscles on his arms as he struck out again and again at the Duke and found to his surprise and fury that each blow was ineffective.

The Duke, after his first astonishment at being attacked, settled down to fight in the experienced manner he had been taught at "Gentleman Jackson's Boxing Academy."

While he was hampered by his coat and his opponent was not, he was aware that he was fighting for his life.

However, because he was slimmer, lighter, and certainly more agile than Jake, the Duke amazingly seemed to hit him frequently while he himself remained unscathed.

Then suddenly, so quickly that she could hardly believe it had happened, the Duke caught Jake with an upper-cut on the point of the chin. His head went back, and as he staggered the Duke hit him again and Jake fell backwards on the road and lay still.

As he did so the second prize-fighter, holding Hibbert at pistol-point, turned his head to watch what had occurred, and then the valet acted.

He brought down his hand stiff as a bar of iron on the man's neck with a blow that was certainly not in the Queensberry Rules but was the chop of death he had learnt from the Chinese on his travels.

The man fell as if pole-axed, but Giōna was only watching the Duke.

There was a smile of satisfaction on his face at having defeated his opponent, and it was then that she was aware that her uncle had drawn his pistol from his right-hand pocket.

"Well done, Your Grace!" he sneered. "But unfortunately Round Two is still to come!"

As he raised his pistol dramatically to bring his aim down on his defenceless victim, Giōna slipped her hand into the other pocket of her uncle's coat and pulled out the other pistol.

Without thinking, without even pausing, she pointed it at his heart and pulled the trigger.

With a resounding explosion the pistol kicked in her hand, and Sir Jarvis, after one moment of immobility, toppled forward and out of the Phaeton onto the road.

As he did so his finger must have tightened on the trigger of his pistol, for it went off, and the second explosion frightened the Duke's horses so that they reared up.

Hibbert desperately tried to keep them under control, but they moved the Phaeton backwards and forwards and in doing so upset Sir Jarvis's horses, which until now had been quietly cropping the grass.

There was a mêlée of horses and wheels, before the Duke sprang into the seat vacated by Sir Jarvis and, taking up the reins, tried to control the terrified animals.

They were bucking and shuffling against each other and only when the two teams had been separated and quieted did Giōna give a cry and put out her hands towards the Duke.

"It is all right," he said soothingly as he put his arm round her.

"I . . . I . . . killed him!" she murmured. "I killed him . . . as he intended to . . . kill you!"

"I realised that."

Then as he tried to pull her closer he saw that she was strapped to the back of the seat.

He did not say anything, but undid the buckle with one hand before he asked quietly:

"You are all right?"

Giōna rested her head against his shoulder, and with an effort she managed to say:

"I am . . . all right."

"Try not to faint now," the Duke said. "I have rather a lot to do!"

It seemed such an odd thing to say that for a moment she forgot about herself as he jumped down from the Phaeton to say to Hibbert:

"What are we to do with this lot?"

Hibbert grinned and his eyes were shining.

"They won't be doing nothing, Your Grace."

He looked down at the ground as he spoke, and the Duke realised that in the confusion after the pistol-shots, the wheels of the Phaeton had passed not only over Sir Jarvis, who was doubtless dead anyway from the shot which Giōna had fired at him, but also over Jake.

The Duke looked at the bodies for a moment, then he said:

"The only people who would be accountable for this mess would be footpads."

"That's just what I was a-thinking myself, Your Grace."

The Duke looked at the man who had been holding up Hibbert and had been felled with the pistol still in his hand.

He then picked up the pistol which had fallen with Sir Jarvis and placed it in Jake's hand.

Then, as if Hibbert realised what was expected of him, he tied the reins in a knot and climbed down.

As they had been together for so long in the war, he knew that his Master would dislike what was obviously the next task in order to leave a misleading but convincing picture to be discovered.

It was therefore the Duke who held the bridle of one of his own horses and one of Sir Jarvis's while Hibbert emptied Sir Jarvis's pockets, took his watch from his waistcoat, a signet-ring from his little finger, and a pearl pin from his cravat.

He then looked at the Duke for orders.

"Stick them in a rabbit-hole in the wood," the latter said.

Hibbert disappeared amongst the trees and the Duke stood watching him go while Giōna was watching him.

It seemed almost a miracle that he had survived, and although she told herself she ought to feel guilty of having murdered a man, all she could do was to thank God fervently in her heart that the Duke was safe.

"Thank . . . You! Thank . . . You!" she whispered, and her prayer sounded like music that might have come from the birds in the trees.

Hibbert came back and the Duke said:

"The sooner we get out of here the better! Somebody will shortly be coming this way."

"I was thinking that myself, Your Grace."

"Then let us waste no more time."

The Duke released the bridle of the horse which had

belonged to Sir Jarvis and, going to the side of the Phaeton, held out his arms.

For a moment Giōna thought she was still too frightened to move.

Then because she knew it would be like touching Heaven to be close to him, she moved towards him and he lifted her from the Phaeton and carried her across to his own.

He set her gently down next to the driving-seat, and as Hibbert jumped up behind, he turned his bays with an expertise that only a Corinthian could achive.

Then they were moving swiftly away from the three dead men lying in the roadway.

They went only a short distance up the road before the Duke drove into a field, and by driving to the other side of the trees brought them back again onto the road which led to the Dower House.

It was only then that he spoke for the first time, aware that Giōna was sitting limply beside him, too exhausted for the moment to be able to think of anything except that he was safe and she no longer need be afraid.

"You are all right?" he asked again.

"You are . . . safe!"

"Thanks to you," he said quietly. "But I will talk to you about that later. Now it is very important that you should do exactly as I tell you."

She looked up at him with wide eyes and he went on:

"Nobody must be aware that either you or I were present at that regrettable and dramatic event that has just taken place."

He drove his horses slowly as he went on:

"In a short time we shall be informed that footpads—and there are quite a number of different types in this neighbourhood—have held up a gentleman who was on his way to call on me at Alverstode House and robbed and killed him."

He paused before he continued slowly:

"It will seem a somewhat complicated crime, because obviously a third man must have got away with the spoils, having quarrelled with his confederates."

Giōna drew in her breath.

"Uncle ... Jarvis," she said with a tremble in her voice, "intended that you should appear to have been ... killed by ... Highwaymen."

"But I am alive, Giōna," the Duke said. "Now you do understand that there must be no question of your knowing anything of what occurred?"

She nodded.

"I know you are intelligent enough to act a part which is going to be difficult for you, but it will save both you and me from a lot of very uncomfortable questioning."

As he spoke, the Duke thought that nothing could be worse than if Giōna was suspected even of being present when her uncle had died, let alone of being instrumental in killing him.

"I am relying on you," he said, "and because I believe you are clever, I am asking you to save us both by a piece of acting which would be greatly applauded if you were on the boards."

"I will ... try."

"I know you will," the Duke said with a smile. "What I want you to do is to walk home from here and say that your uncle only took you with him a short distance because he wished to speak to you alone."

"That man you ... knocked down ... picked me up from the ... bottom of the stairs and ... carried me out to the ... Phaeton."

"Who saw it happen?" the Duke asked sharply.

"Only Simpson."

"Tell him it was a joke, the sort of thing your uncle thought funny. You must be convincing."

He took her hand and kissed it.

"I will see you later today," he said. "Remember,

everything depends on your appearing as if nothing untoward had happened."

He brought the horses to a standstill and Giōna saw that the lodge-gate was only about twenty yards ahead.

"You are . . . safe," she said in a very low voice, as if she was confirming it to herself rather than to him.

"And so are you, for the rest of your life," the Duke replied quietly.

Their eyes met and it was difficult to look away.

Then Giōna climbed down from the Phaeton and started to walk along the road to the gate.

She was aware as she did so that the Duke was turning his horses once more and driving back along the road.

But as she walked on Giōna was conscious of those words that repeated themselves again and again in the beat of her heart:

"He is . . . safe! He is . . . safe!"

Chapter Seven

"I think I will go upstairs and rest," the Duchess said as she and Giōna walked from the Dining-Room.

"I think you . . . would be . . . wise . . . Ma'am."

Giōna spoke in a hesitating voice which made the Duchess look at her sharply.

"A rest would doubtless do you good," she said. "You are looking as pale as when you first came here."

"I think . . . it is the . . . heat," Giōna answered quickly. "I will go into the . . . garden and get some . . . fresh air."

"Yes, do that," the Duchess agreed. "Perhaps my grandson will be here at tea-time to tell us what has delayed him."

Giōna did not say anything, and when the Duchess had walked slowly up the stairs she turned and went onto the terrace.

She had taxed her self-control almost to breaking point in playing the part the Duke had demanded of her.

When she had got back to the Dower House, Simpson was hovering in the Hall in an agitated state.

"What happened to you, Miss Giōna?" he asked. "Why were you carried off in that extraordinary way? I were a-wondering what to do about it."

With a superhuman effort, Giōna managed a light laugh.

"It was just a joke on the part of my uncle," she said. "He meant to surprise me, and succeeded. When we had gone a short way he told me I could walk back. It is the sort of trick he thinks is funny."

The anxiety in Simpson's old eyes cleared.

"So that's what it was all about, Miss!" he exclaimed. "I was a-fearing all sorts of strange things might have happened to you, and were just about to send out the grooms to search for you!"

"There is nothing stranger than that I have got my slippers dusty," Giōna replied. "I will go upstairs and change them."

She went up to her bedroom and to her relief there was nobody there, the housemaids having finished tidying it.

She sat down in a chair and for a moment the room seemed to swim round her and a darkness came up from the floor.

Then she told herself that the Duke trusted her, that it was far too soon to collapse, and that she must act her part so skilfully that, as he intended, nobody would have the slightest suspicion of what had happened.

But as the morning progressed she could only think that she should be more ashamed of having killed a man, even though in doing so she had saved the Duke.

But was he safe from scandal and from the gossip which would inevitably involve him if by some mischance anybody learnt what had really happened?

She was well aware what a story the chatterers in the Social World would make of the fact that the Duke had fought Sir Jarvis and that his daughter wished to marry Lucien, who had not proposed.

And worst of all, she, Sir Jarvis's niece, had somehow become entangled with the Duke of Alverstode.

What would be thought, what would be said, and

what the newspapers would print whirled round in Giōna's mind until she knew that the only thing which could dispel the feeling that she might go insane with anxiety was to see the Duke.

She began to count the hours until there was a chance of his appearing.

She had to calculate how long it would be before somebody found the three dead men lying in the road, and if—which was likely—it was one of the Duke's employees, he would report it first to the Duke's house before there was any question of telling the Magistrates.

Even so, Giōna was certain that the Duke would somehow keep free from all the consternation and speculation and would come to luncheon.

She found herself listening for the wheels of his Phaeton drawing up outside the front door, and it was only with the greatest difficulty that she did not run to look out the windows every five minutes to see if there was any sign of his horses coming down the drive.

When at last there was the sound of hoofs on the gravel, it was only a groom carrying a note to the Duchess.

The Duchess, who by this time was downstairs, read it and handed it to Giōna.

For a moment the Duke's strong, upright writing seemed to swim in front of her eyes, then she read:

Forgive Me, Grandmama, if I cannot have Luncheon with You as I had hoped, but I am detained by some tiresome Business. However, I hope I may be with You sometime during the Afternoon.

> *I remain,*
> *Your affectionate and respectful*
> *Grandson,*
> *Valerian.*

"'Some tiresome business,'" Giōna repeated beneath her breath, and prayed that he was not making too light of something which was very serious.

Now as she walked amongst the roses, thinking of the Duke, a sudden thought made her feel as if she had been struck a heavy blow.

If in fact no serious difficulties arose from Sir Jarvis's death, not only would the Duke be safe but so would she! In which case there would be no need for him to protect her any further.

She had been so terrified of her uncle and he had menaced her for so long that it was only now that she was gradually realising that because he was dead, she was a free person and could go anywhere she liked.

If this had happened to her when she was at Stamford Towers she knew she would have felt like a caged bird who could suddenly fly up into the sky. But now she knew that in becoming free she would lose the Duke.

He had taken care of her and helped her to escape and brought her here to safety only because he had felt sorry for her! And she was aware, without his telling her, that he loathed cruelty of any sort.

She was sure that she meant nothing to him as a woman and that only his sense of justice and his compassion had impelled him to save her from degradation and death.

Now he would no longer be interested!

Instead of feeling happy about her future, she could only see the loneliness and emptiness of it.

She would have money, for the Duke would see to it that what her father had left would be restored to her. Then he would return to his friends, his sports, and the responsibilities of his distinguished position, while she would be left with nothing but an aching heart.

'I love him!' she thought. 'But what could my love mean to him when any of the famous beauties who surround the Regent can be his for the asking?'

She had heard of his successes from the Duchess, who liked to talk of the scandals of the *Beau Monde* and without really meaning to had said many things that enlightened Giōna as to her grandson's attractions.

Her comments on what appeared in the Social Columns of *The Times* and *The Morning Post* often brought strange stabs of pain, although Giōna had not at first realised why she was distressed.

"I see that Lady Mary Crewson was in attendance at Buckingham Palace this week," the Duchess had remarked yesterday. "I always found her a tiresome woman, but she is very beautiful. I suppose I can understand what Valerian saw in her, although his interest did not last long."

The Engagement Columns always evoked revealing remarks.

"So the Duke of Northumberland's daughter is engaged at last!" the Dowager had exclaimed one morning. "I thought she was still wearing the willow for Valerian. She would have made him a very suitable wife, but he would not look at her!"

Women and more women! Giōna was sure they were all as beautiful as the sunrise, or as the moonlight flooding the valley when she and the Duke had sat together on the fallen tree.

Without realising where she was going, Giōna found her way to the arbour and sat down on the seat.

She tried to steel herself against what she was sure the Duke would say to her when finally he arrived.

She wondered why he was taking so long.

Perhaps the Chief Constable suspected that the scene they had set to suggest a quarrel amongst footpads was not genuine. If he suspected the Duke of having killed her uncle, then she would have to clear him by telling the truth.

She was certain that the Duke initially would try to take the blame, but that was something she could not allow him to do.

Under an interrogation the whole sordid story would be revealed, the tale of her uncle's cruelty would strip her naked to the public gaze, and she would never again be able to hold up her head.

If, on the other hand, everything worked out as the Duke had planned, then he would say good-bye, perhaps suggesting that she could stay a little longer with his grandmother.

But she could hardly remain an uninvited guest forever, and in fact from today she must start planning her own future.

Perhaps she would rent a house in London and could pay some respectable elderly woman or a widow to chaperone her. Or perhaps it would be better to leave England and return to a life of travelling restlessly to any part of the world that was not at war.

She would be alone, completely alone, and she knew that in the future no man would ever attract her, for having given her love once, it was no longer hers to give again.

She wanted to cry at the misery of her own thoughts. Then she told herself that if the Duke found her in tears he would despise her for not being able to carry out his orders more competently.

Already his grandmother suspected that something was wrong because she was so pale, and perhaps Simpson had not really believed the story she had told him.

Because she was disturbed and upset, everything seemed ominous and frightening as the difficulties, the problems, and the questions closed in upon her.

She suddenly felt almost as if she must scream aloud, when she looked up and the Duke was there!

He had approached without her hearing him, and now he stood just outside the arbour, though for one moment she thought he was just a figment of her imagination.

Her heart seemed to stop beating before she sprang to her feet and with a cry ran towards him.

"What has... happened? Why have... you been so... long? Is... anything... wrong?"

The questions seemed to tumble incoherently from her lips and she could not control them.

Without thinking, without even meaning to do so, Gióna held on to him almost as if he might escape and leave her without replying.

"Everything is all right," the Duke said soothingly. "I am sorry if I have been a long time in coming to you, but it was unavoidable."

The calmness of his voice made Gióna look up at him searchingly, and her eyes seemed to fill the whole of her small face as she asked:

"They... believed it? They... accepted that it was... footpads who... killed Uncle Jarvis?"

The way she spoke was so unsteady that the Duke put his arm round her as if to support her.

"The Military are already searching for the murderer, although they admit that without any idea of what he may look like, they have little hope of capturing him."

He smiled slightly as he spoke. Then he said very quietly:

"There is no need for you to worry any more. You saved my life, Gióna."

He felt her tremble as if she remembered the moment when she had thought he must die and it was still too vivid to be anything but an agonising terror.

"Forget it," he added, "and let me thank you instead, because I am in fact very grateful indeed for being here with you."

There was a note in his voice that made her look at him wonderingly, but without the fear that had been there before.

The Duke gently pulled her a little closer. Then he said:

"I have been wondering as I came here how I could express my happiness at being alive, and this is the way I wish to do it."

As he spoke his lips came down on hers.

Just for a moment Giōna could hardly believe it was happening, then as the Duke took possession of her mouth she knew that this was what she had longed for!

This was the only way it was possible to express the love that had made her yearn for him and pray for him all through the darkness of her misery and despair.

Now she felt as if her whole body came pulsatingly alive and there was no longer darkness but a light that enveloped them both yet came from their hearts.

The Duke's kiss was at first very gentle, as if he was afraid to frighten her.

Then as he felt the softness of her lips and the quiver that went through her at his touch, he pulled her closer still and his mouth became more insistent, more demanding.

He knew as he felt her respond that the feeling he had awakened in her and felt in himself was different from anything he had known before, but he could not explain it in words.

He knew only that everything about Giōna was different from all the other women who had attracted and intrigued him but inevitably sooner or later had bored him.

What he felt for her was not only physical, although he certainly wanted her as a woman, but she also aroused something entirely spiritual in him.

It was a secret ideal which he had always been aware of and which lay at the back of his thinking, but which he had never shared with anybody else.

Now as he felt the same adoration on her lips that he had seen in her eyes, he knew that because she believed in him he would strive to live up to her idea that he was Apollo bringing light and healing to the world.

It flashed through his mind that there was a great deal they could do together to prevent other monsters like Sir Jarvis from perpetrating cruelty on those who were too weak to defend themselves.

Although the slave-trade had been abolished by an Act of Parliament twelve years ago, there was still slavery in many other walks of life, which, although it might have a different name, still meant the strong exploiting and degrading of the weak.

Then as he raised his head Giōna murmured:

"I love . . . you!"

As the Duke heard the irrepressible note of rapture in her voice and saw by the expression in her eyes what she felt for him, he knew he was the most fortunate man in the world.

"I love you too, my precious!" he replied. "And nobody shall ever frighten or ill-treat you again."

Her face was transformed with happiness, then as she gave an inarticulate little murmur, he said:

"I will look after you, and now there is nothing to prevent us from being married as soon as possible."

"M-married?"

It was difficult to articulate the word.

"There is nobody to whom we must apply for permission," the Duke said, "and the only Guardian you will have in the future, my lovely one, will be your husband, who will be me!"

"Are you . . . are you . . . really asking me to . . . marry you?" Giōna whispered.

"It is not really a question," the Duke replied, "for I will not allow you to say 'No.' I want you, my darling, and it is difficult to tell you how much."

"I love you until you . . . fill the whole world . . . and the sky . . . and there is . . . nothing else but you!" Giōna said. "But you ought to . . . marry somebody very . . . much more . . . important."

"I intend to marry you," the Duke said firmly, "and the person who will approve of my choice and who matters to me more than any of my other relatives is my grandmother."

"You are . . . sure? Quite sure of that?" Giōna asked.

"Very sure," the Duke smiled, "but it is really of no consequence what Grandmama or anybody else thinks. I love you, and that is the only thing that matters to me."

"And to . . . me!" Giōna cried. "But are you certain, really certain in your heart that you . . . want me for- . . . ever?"

"For ever and ever as I have never wanted anybody else," the Duke confirmed. "Oh, my darling, do you not realise how sweet and beautiful you are?"

She turned her face up to his and he looked down at her with an expression in his eyes that made Giōna's heart turn over in her breast.

It was the look she had longed to see, and now she knew that, unbelievable though it might seem, the Duke loved her as she loved him.

She had a feeling that what they were saying to each other had been ordained long before they had met or had even been born.

He would say it was fate or the gods that had brought them together, but she knew she had been right in thinking that like Apollo he had brought light into the darkness and misery of her world when there had been nothing but pain and the expectation of dying.

As if he knew what she was thinking, the Duke drew her closer to him and said:

"Never again, and this is a vow, my dearest heart, will I allow you to be unhappy or afraid. Never again will you suffer or feel alone and without love."

"How can you say such wonderful things to me?" Giōna asked.

"They are easy to say," the Duke answered, "because you are the most wonderful thing that has ever happened to me."

"That is what I should be saying to you," Giōna said passionately. "You came to . . . me when I was . . . in despair, and now I want to... kneel at your feet and pour out my love as a... thank-offering."

The Duke gave a little laugh as he answered:

"I will not have you kneeling at my feet so long as I can hold you in my arms, my beautiful one. But I want you to pour out your love because it is the most precious thing I have ever known, and I need it and want it."

He did not wait for her answer but was kissing her again with possessive, demanding kisses that seemed to Giōna to hold the fire of the sun.

She felt an echoing flame within herself, and as the Duke drew her closer and closer still, she thought that the wonder and glory of it seemed to leap in a shaft of crimson towards the sky.

It was so wonderful, so ecstatic, that when finally his kiss ended she turned to look up at him wonderingly, as if she stared at the glory of the Divine.

At the same time she was aware that the Duke's heart was beating violently, as hers was, and they were both a little breathless.

"I want you!" he said, and his voice was deep. "I want you, my darling, in a thousand ways, but only when you are my wife will I be able to show you how much you really matter to me."

He touched her cheek with his fingers, running them along the line of her chin, then down the side of her soft neck.

It gave Giōna a sensation she had never known before and made her breath come quickly between her lips.

"You make me... feel... very strange," she whispered.

"What is it like?" the Duke asked.

"Like... like... a shaft of... sunshine."

The Duke smiled.

"My darling, you are so sweet and unspoilt!"

"Are... you laughing at me... because I am... ignorant?"

"Only adoring you because your innocence is what I never thought to find, but it also excites me!"

"I . . . excite . . . you?"

"More than I dare tell you at this moment."

He felt her draw in her breath and he said:

"I will ask you again—how soon will you marry me?"

"Now! This . . . second!" Giōna cried.

He laughed gently.

"That is what I want you to say, and so let us go and talk to Grandmama, for it will cure her rheumatism and make her twenty years younger if we are married here in her house and she can make all the arrangements."

"I am sure she will do that . . . if only she will . . . agree that I am . . . good enough for you."

"I think she had the idea that you might marry Lucien."

"Lucien?" Giōna exclaimed in astonishment. "But how ridiculous! He is only a boy."

"I am rather afraid that you may think I am too old for you."

"I think that you are perfect . . . the most wonderful man that ever existed, and when one is in love . . . I do not think that . . . age matters one way or the other."

"That is true," the Duke agreed, "and when we are together, my darling love, we are the same age because we think the same and feel the same, and in the future, because of our love, we will grow more and more like each other."

"That is true . . . I am sure it is true!" Giōna cried. "But will my love be . . . enough?"

She looked away from him before she said in a low voice:

"You do realise that I am very . . . ignorant about all the things that interest you in . . . England because I have never . . . lived in this country? I shall make mistakes . . . and perhaps you will be . . . ashamed of me."

The Duke smiled and pulled her close to him again.

"You are insulting me by telling me I am very insular," he said. "But I think we both agree that in our minds and our imaginations we can encircle the world, in which case what does it matter what happens in London if we are touching the peaks of the Himalayas or sailing over the Red Sea?"

Giōna laughed and he thought it was the prettiest sound he had ever heard.

"Only . . . you would say . . . something like . . . that."

"Actually, I am rather surprised at myself," the Duke admitted. "I am not as a rule given to poetic fantasy!"

She looked up at him and he knew what she was thinking by the expression in her eyes.

"You are right," he said softly, "it is love that has changed me, love for you, my precious little goddess with the Greek nose, love which makes me feel entirely different from any way I have felt before. I shall never again be surprised at anything I say, think, or do."

"That is . . . how I love you," Giōna murmured, "only . . . please . . . because I want to be with you . . . and you to teach me . . . let us be married very . . . very quickly."

"That is one thing about which we are in complete agreement!" the Duke said firmly.

He put his arm round her shoulders as they walked together back to the house, then as if he could not help himself he drew her almost roughly against him and once again he was kissing her.

Now his lips were demanding and fiercely, insistently possessive, as if his need of her spirit or her soul made him attempt to draw it from her lips and make it his.

The fire in him awakened a fire within Giōna, and she felt as if they were both being consumed by their love until it carried them into the sky.

They were one with the stars under which they had once sat and talked, one with the sun, crimson and gold, which moving round the world and whose light was never extinguished.

Shining, dazzling, brilliant and compelling, it was part of God.

A shaft of it joined Giōna with the Duke to bind them together for eternity.

ABOUT THE AUTHOR

BARBARA CARTLAND, the world's most famous romantic novelist, who is also an historian, playwright, lecturer, political speaker and television personality, has now written over 300 books.

She has also had many historical works published and has written four autobiographies as well as the biographies of her mother and that of her brother Ronald Cartland, who was the first Member of Parliament to be killed in W.W. II. This book has a preface by Sir Winston Churchill and has just been republished with an introduction by Sir Arthur Bryant.

Barbara Cartland has sold 200 million books over the world, more than half of these in the U.S.A. She broke the world record in 1975 by writing twenty-three books and the four subsequent years with 20, 21, 23 and 24. In addition her album of love songs has just been published, sung with the Royal Philharmonic Orchestra.

Barbara Cartland, who is a Dame of the Order of St. John of Jerusalem, has championed the cause for old people and founded the first Romany Gypsy Camp in the world.

Barbara Cartland is deeply interested in Vitamin Therapy and is President of the British National Association for Health. Her book the *Magic of Honey* has sold in millions all over the world.

She has a magazine *The World of Romance* and her Barbara Cartland Romantic World Tours will, in conjunction with British Airways, carry travelers to England, Egypt, India, France, Germany and Turkey.

Barbara Cartland

The world's bestselling author of romantic fiction. Her stories are always captivating tales of intrigue, adventure and love.

☐	13830	THE DAWN OF LOVE	$1.75
☐	14503	THE LIONESS AND THE LILY	$1.75
☐	13942	LUCIFER AND THE ANGEL	$1.75
☐	14084	OLA AND THE SEA WOLF	$1.75
☐	14133	THE PRUDE AND THE PRODIGAL	$1.75
☐	13032	PRIDE AND THE POOR PRINCESS	$1.75
☐	13984	LOVE FOR SALE	$1.75
☐	14248	THE GODDESS AND THE GAIETY GIRL	$1.75
☐	14360	SIGNPOST TO LOVE	$1.75
☐	14361	FROM HELL TO HEAVEN	$1.75
☐	14585	LOVE IN THE MOON	$1.95
☐	13985	LOST LAUGHTER	$1.75
☐	14750	DREAMS DO COME TRUE	$1.95
☐	14902	WINGED MAGIC	$1.95
☐	14922	A PORTRAIT OF LOVE	$1.95

Buy them at your local bookstore or use this handy coupon for ordering:

Bantam Books, Inc., Dept. BC2, 414 East Golf Road, Des Plaines, Ill. 60016

Please send me the books I have checked above. I am enclosing $_____ (please add $1.00 to cover postage and handling). Send check or money order —no cash or C.O.D.'s please.

Mr/Mrs/Miss_____

Address_____

City_____ State/Zip_____

BC2—11/81

Please allow four to six weeks for delivery. This offer expires 4/82.

<u>SAVE $2.00</u> ON YOUR NEXT BOOK ORDER!

BANTAM BOOKS🐓

Shop-at-Home ─────
Catalog

Now you can have a complete, up-to-date catalog of Bantam's inventory of over 1,600 titles—including hard-to-find books.

And, you can <u>save $2.00</u> on your next order by taking advantage of the money-saving coupon you'll find in this illustrated catalog. Choose from fiction and non-fiction titles, including mysteries, historical novels, westerns, cookbooks, romances, biographies, family living, health, and more. You'll find a description of most titles. Arranged by categories, the catalog makes it easy to find your favorite books and authors and to discover new ones.

So don't delay—send for this shop-at-home catalog and save money on your next book order.

Just send us your name and address and 50¢ to defray postage and handling costs.

BANTAM BOOKS, INC.
Dept. FC, 414 East Golf Road, Des Plaines, Ill. 60016

Mr./Mrs./Miss_____
(please print)
Address_____

City_____State_____Zip_____

Do you know someone who enjoys books? Just give us their names and addresses and we'll send them a catalog too at no extra cost!

Mr./Mrs./Miss_____

Address_____

City_____State_____Zip_____

Mr./Mrs./Miss_____

Address_____

City_____State_____Zip_____

FC—9/81